A GRIM & REAPER NETHERWORLD TALE

# VENGEANCE Born

# L.C. SON

**Vengeance Born**

Copyright © 2023 by L.C. Son
ISBN: 979-8-9862237-6-6



This book and all parts of the Netherworld and the Beautiful Nightmare Universe and its
collection are works of fiction. Names, characters, businesses, places, events, and incidents
are either the products of the author's imagination or used in a fictional manner. Any
resemblance to actual persons, living or dead, is purely coincidental.

www.LCSonBooks.com

Cover Design by Mibl Art
Illustrated Character Art by Linds
Formatting by Megan J. Parker-Squiers
Editing by Alexa Thomas at The Fiction Fix

# Contents

# Content Guide

This book contains content suitable for mature adults aged 18+. It includes sexual situations, discussions of grief, death, attempted rape, and sexual abuse.

The above is not exhaustive. Additional provided at the following: http://www.lcsonbooks.com/vengeance-born.html
Please consider before reading.

# Dedication

*Stop running from your shadow.*
*Embrace it.*
*It takes a lot of strength to reflect the light.*

*~LC~*

# NETHERWORLD GLOSSARY
## UNDERSTAND THE DIALECT OF THE DARK

**NETHER-** Void of life

**NIGHT-** Ancient deity of darkness

**PURGIA-** Place of purgatory

**FATES-** Those who see into the future

**FESTIVUS-** Day of the Dead

**CHASM-** A dark void

**MIRTH-** The opposite of gladness; a bleak place of void and darkness

**EXCRESCO-** To compel to enlarge or grow

**DEAD-AND-WAKE-** A violent hit or blow causing one to appear as dead

**DEATH DEALER-** One responsible for executing end of life orders

**UNDERWORLD-** Final repose of wandering where Hades rules

**EARTHBOUND REALM-** Where mortals, vampires, wolves and those bound to life reside

**SOLEIL-** Central site where all Purgian garb is magically fashioned

# THELIOS

**Species- Grim Lord & Death Dealer**

**Powers- Dark Chasm, Portal Magic, Shadow Magic**

# A GRIM

## LORNA-SYDNEY
### Species- Specter
### Powers- Dark Suspension, Wraith Shadow

# CHAPTER 1

## *Thelios*

**D**eath. Even among us in the Netherworld, it is a mysterious and ominous power—a power so strong, so gripping, that it winds itself into you until you're left with nothing of yourself.

That's where I come in.

As the resident Grim of Purgia, the place where all lie in wait for their final judgment, I alone carry within myself the mirth of darkness, void of life. The very essence of nothingness rests in the murky chasm of my power.

And while it may be a void of whatever life is found here in the Netherworld, it is still only a fragment of the power of death itself.

It is for that reason that a line stretching beyond what even my eyes can see stands before me now: because no one wants to die. Immortality is the enviable, albeit unattainable, presence that eludes us all. While we may live more than ten times the lifespan of mortals in the earthbound realm, all creatures, both mortal and supernatural, desire the one thing of which we are incapable: possessing our own souls.

In fact, some would rather give themselves to my mirth, which is their right, than to board the ships to an uncertain finality on the shores of the Underworld, where Hades awaits. There, Hades uses souls for his own gain, leaving those who remain to wander in the void of his keep while he usurps their power.

Many would rather slip into nothingness than grant Hades such a prize.

And so, they stand before me now.

"Next!" Dane shouts to my left, waving the line forward.

I sigh, watching as a feeble, yet stout and heavily-bearded, troll ambles toward my table. I already know where this is going. The man will beg for his life, promising some grand gesture as I gather him into my scythe, only for me to end up with nothing in return.

"Name." Dane's tone is flat as he stares up at the man, prepared to write his name on the scroll. If there's one thing we pride ourselves on in the Netherworld, it's recordkeeping. While Hades allows us a modicum of autonomy by taking a small percentage of those destined for the Underworld into my mirth, he wants all souls accounted for.

There are only three ways to escape the Underworld:

Be handpicked by the Prince of Purgia, Kharon the Ferryman, to remain as a resident of his province.

Be chosen by lottery, which I also manage, to become a resident.

Or vacate your soul either via my mirth by freewill, or reaped by Roark if found in vagrancy.

There are no other options.

The bearded troll's hand shakes as he quietly mumbles something too faint to comprehend.

"Louder, old man!" Dane shouts, his patience waning.

I don't look at the troll. Instead, my eyes shift upward toward the black gates—there's rumbling in the courtyard.

"Let us through!" a distinct female voice clips through the darkness.

"You are not permitted inside!" Calis, the chief guard of my citadel, bites back. "Only those chosen for high court may enter. All others remain at the disposal of the lower magistrates."

Normally, I would ignore the usual grumbles in the courtyard, but a small whimper, like that of a child, catches my attention. Children are a rarity in the Netherworld, and even more so are those set to board the ships to the Underworld.

"I demand an audience with the Grim lord!" the same female voice shouts again. This time, it's followed by a menacing snarl, a singsong lilt weaved into her words. It's soothing but violent, and I like it.

But there's something else—a magnetism I've never known tugs at the heartless hole in my chest. Vertigo sets in as the black gates invert like a boomerang until I'm left with nothing but the view of a woman wearing a dark cape. I shake my head, hopeful to ward off the dizzying spell. Looking up, I notice a small soul by her side, likely the child I heard earlier.

I stand from behind my table, and Dane's eyes grow wide in surprise. Even he is surprised by my response. I am not easily rattled, but this woman...something about her disturbs me.

"My–my name is—" A quivering voice from the other side of the table reclaims my attention. It's the bearded troll. I don't care what his name is or where he's from; he's wasted enough of my time.

Without warning, I lift my scythe. *Into darkness,* I whisper as a chasm funnel forms at my side, instantly drawing the troll into my dark flume. I close my eyes as raw currents of electricity rivet through me, absorbing his essence into my own. Still, I feel nothing. Just as I assumed, the troll had little to offer.

"Stay back!" Calis yells once more, and my eyes pop open, only to see the woman and child closer than before. "If I have to tell you again, I'll board you on the ship to Hades myself!"

Snarling once more, the woman turns to Calis, squaring her shoulders, daring him to respond. "You won't lay a hand on me!" she grits through her teeth. "I must speak with the Grim lord!"

As Calis lifts his brawny arms, I know what comes next: he intends to strike her into a dead-and-wake, a blow so strong that she'll appear as dead until she wakes hours later. By that time, he would have her shackled and bundled aboard the ship to the Underworld.

I watch as if time stood still, marveling at the mysterious woman demanding to see me. Although her hooded cloak gives me nothing more than her voluptuous silhouette and a pair of legs that curve just outside her covering, something about her lulls me into something akin to peace.

Still, the woman does not flinch. Either she accepts her fate, or she devises some sinister will in her mind—which one, I do not know.

What I do know is that I must have her.

And so I shall.

Hala squeezes her small arms around my waist, grinding her teeth, fearful of the blow we'll both receive from the Grim lord's guard. I, though, keep my eyes trained on the burly, dark haired man before me.

I could lift my cloak, show him everything a wraith-like soul like me has to offer, but I know better. Doing so would likely enrage not only this lowly guard, but the Grim whose mercy I need most.

Correction. *We* need.

The guard's large, muscular arm hurls toward me in slow motion, and I watch closely as thick hairs stand on his forearm. They're more in line with those of nocturnal creatures like porcupines, rather than those with fur, but I don't fear the needle-point blow destined to tear into my flesh.

No. That is the least of my worries.

What I fear is letting my little sister become a lottery prize of that savage, Purcival. Many believe only the high courts oversee the grand lottery held at Festivus, but very few know of the low-court underbelly lottery market.

Scalpers like Purcival trick poor souls like our father to gamble where the stakes are high. Not only did Purcival trade our lottery for his own gain, but he sold my father's soul to the black ships of Hades—the ships even the Ferryman himself doesn't steer. Now, with Purcival's duplicitous nature, I fear his intentions toward my young sister.

Claiming me as a soiled wench, Purcival set his wicked sights on Hala from the day her bosom blossomed. He desires to make her his personal milking wench or some other lascivious tool for his depraved pleasures.

So, here I stand, willing to take whatever blow I must to ensure my sister's safety. She is all that matters.

I wince, tightening my eyes while sucking in a breath as I feel the heat of his arm whip through the wind at the side of my face, but it doesn't land.

Peering through my hood, I'm surprised to see a bone-white hand now wrapped around the guard's wrist, holding it steady in mid-air.

It's the Grim lord.

Only the side view of a skeletal-painted face with bright green eyes glares in my direction. There's a haughty curl to his lips, his raised brow letting me know I owe a debt.

Dropping to my knees, I pull Hala down with me. "Thank you, my lord," I groan, hating even the sight of me groveling before any man.

"Don't thank me yet," a lush, heavy voice sweeps over me like the wind.

"Please, my lord," I continue, my face still lowered to the ground. Hala shrieks at my side, squeezing me tighter as two black snakes coil around the Grim lord's ankles and slither up his legs to hide beneath his thick black gown. I firm my grip on my sister's hand, hoping to calm her. "We beg for your aid."

"They are a matter for the lower court, my lord," the guard quickly answers.

A low tremor rumbles through the Grim lord, but he says nothing. His thick gown rustles, and I feel him leaning over me. Long, boney fingers stretch out from the sleeves of his cloak as his hand finds my chin. His touch is gentler than I'd expect as he slowly lifts my face to meet his.

I've never been more thankful for our practice of remaining hooded. Being what we are, only our true mates are permitted to see our face in full. It's been eons since I've removed my hood—so long, in fact, I'd barely recognize my own face.

I can only see through the thin veil of cloth that has forever been my covering. It's a good thing that while I can see out, no one can see in.

Still, the Grim lord is careful not to let his hands wander further than my chin. Even for a Grim lord as renowned as he, I fear what the sight of me could do to him. More so, I fear the sight of me would repulse him. He'd gladly send me to the shores of Hades himself.

"Well then," he begins in such a low tone, I strain to hear it.

"Yes, my lord?" I answer, my lip quivering.

"You said something about begging."

My breath hitches. He's making me eat my words in front of everyone. No doubt many are furious I've garnered his attention for my own, but I can't worry about them now. I must do what I came to do: save my sister. If I lose my own life in the process, so be it.

"My lord, we, my sister and I, seek your mercy."

A hearty laugh rolls through the courtyard. With the way the onlookers carry about, you would think I was the court jester.

The Grim lord's shoulder's shake with amusement. "You are Nether, dear one. Even you know there is no grace or mercy found in these lands. Dare I say, not even in Purgia."

The laughter grows louder, and I do what I can to make sure he hears me. Sitting back on my knees, I rear my shoulders back and lift my head. "But my lord," I exclaim, reclaiming his attention as a sly skeletal grin hovers once more at the side of his mouth. He raises a fist, quieting the crowd. "There is yet mercy in your chasm, is there not?"

He turns away from me, motioning for two of his guards. I suppose he no longer finds me amusing.

"Or perhaps there is mercy somewhere–anywhere—in your court? Your galley, perhaps? *Your bedchamber?*" The last phrase is a whisper; I've run out of options. "Please, I beg of you!"

Throwing myself at his feet, I tug at the hem of his cloak. I know it isn't permitted to handle an esteemed member of the High Court like this, but I've run out of options. The cape of my hood flies back as I lay outstretched before him.

I'm not sure if he'll throw me into his chasm as he did the troll before me, but even that would be a better fate than Hades or Purcival. As long as Hala and I are together, that is all that matters.

His large green eyes beam down at me as he bites his lip. Devious intentions dance behind his eyes as they land square on my breasts, nearly popping out of my corset as my father's heirloom sways between my cleavage.

"Mmm..." he hums, rubbing his boney hands together. "I like the way you beg."

# CHAPTER 3
## *Thelios*

Once again, I'm mesmerized.

This time, however, it's not from the vertigo of the black gates. Instead, it's the view of this mysteriously perfect creature grasping at my ankle. I've never seen more beautiful begging in my entire existence.

It's not just the sight of her luscious breast spilling out so perfectly before me that catches my attention. Rather, it's the trinket looming between them that stops me in my tracks.

From what I gather of this woman and the child clinging to her side, they are Specter folk—wraith kind, bound in cloaks, lest their hallowing glare damn you into a hell-like state. It's been years since I've seen one up close since, rumor has it, the wicked Changelings laid waste to the Specters and very few remain. They may be all that is left of their kind.

"My lord?" the woman whispers, her full lips, the color of pomegranate, curling upward as she cranes her neck toward me.

As I offer my hand, she places her petite, yet frightfully pale, palm in mine. I help her from the ground, and she stands upright with the child nestled under her arm.

Trailing my hand along her chin, I slowly twine my fingers around the shiny ring hanging on a silver cord just above her bustline. I do my best to push aside the desire to run my boney palm over the pillowy soft mounds tempting my resolve.

I don't know how she obtained such an ornament, but I find it curious that something of Grim origin would be found on a Specter, of all folk.

Dropping my hand so as not to bring undue attention to the rare find adorned on such a perfect vessel, I allow my palm to squeeze at her breast, just enough to make others think I only want her for one reason.

She grunts, to my surprise, as my thumb grazes the imprint of her nipple, and the sound makes my dick jolt.

*Shit. Fuck.* I can't let the crowd see me aroused in this manner.

Quickly yanking my hand to my side, I turn away from her and back to Dane, trying to catch my breath. Looking at his cycloptic-orge face is quite enough to tame the beast bucking beneath my cloak.

"Mark this one for my…" I pause, my eyes searching around the courtyard. I know I must choose wisely. There are many willing to offer more than their soul just to abide in my chasm. Most would do anything to avoid wandering soulless around the Underworld at the hand of Hades.

"Sire?" Dane asks, pen in hand, ready to write down whatever I command.

"My bedchamber," I continue.

The courtyard splinters into whispers. Legends of my *escapades* are renowned. Male and female alike clamor for the chance to lay with me. The rumors of my vigor run far and wide throughout Purgia. While some say I merely take the leftovers off the Prince's hand, even more are curious as to how such a hollow soul such as myself can leave one to climax over four watches of the night.

"Ah yes. To your harem, my lord. I shall call for Sabine to—"

"No!" I lash, whipping my head hard over my shoulder. "I said to my bedchamber. This one will not align with the harem. At least, not yet." I want to say I want her all to myself, but I dare not.

Dane doesn't flinch; he's grown accustomed to my outbursts. "And what of the small one, my lord?" Dane points a thick, furry finger at the child still clinging tight to the woman's side.

Damn it. I almost forgot about that one.

Quivering, the youngling perches near the woman's bosom. A small, round face, with shockingly rosy cheeks and pink lips peers underneath her hood and from beneath the woman's hold.

"Please, my lord," the woman begins, once more assuring her voice is heard. "This is my sister. I am all she has."

"I assure you, my bedchamber is no place for a child." I grimace at the thought. Besides, children are an enigma to me. Most in the Netherworld, like myself, are made from the soil of our origin. I am from the Isle of Mirth, birthed from Chaos himself, as is the case with most Nether-folk. Still, there remain some who procreate, but life is a rare commodity, not one that is highly sought. We have no need for such things such as children.

Still, I must do something with her. "Issue her to Pella's council." The Viridian Sprite, and ward of the Prince, is probably the only one in the high court to welcome a child.

"Yes, my lord," Dane says, marking her in the tablet.

"But do tell Pella that once she is of age, she may proceed to the Prince's harem."

"No, my lord!" the woman gasps, stepping out. Her hand reaches forward, but when I offer only a scowl in return, she retracts it. "Please, sire, not the harem. She is just a child!"

I've grown tired of her pleas. In fact, if it weren't for that trinket at her neck, I'd throw her into a chasm and never think about her again. *Or at least, I would try.* I could tear it from her throat, but that would only draw attention to its importance, and since I am the only one here who knows how valuable it is, it's best I keep her close until I know more.

"Enough!" I growl, screeching aloud so my skeletal grin forms into a ghastly scream, revealing only the darkness of my being. The entirety of the courtyard falls silent, and many drop to their knees or bow at the waist. Everyone, that is, except the woman. Even the child laments reverently at her side. The woman, however, holds her ground. *Impressive.*

"I will not leave my sister to a wench's fate," the woman announces, as if she had a choice.

My shadow wraps around the courtyard until I am once more in front of her. "No, you will leave her to any fate at my whim. Unless, of course, you'd rather board the boats."

The woman's lips part in protest, but the young child tugs her sleeve. "No sister," she begins, and I am surprised at the full-bodied tone of her voice. "I am no child, my lord, but I am not quite a woman. Until the day comes, I shall wait for the Prince, as shall be my duty, so as long as my sister, Lorna Sydney, remains safe here in Purgia."

"Hala, no!" the woman, *Lorna Sydney*, protests, and I watch two black teardrops race to her chin.

"Wise words, child. Wise indeed." With that, I bang the rod of my scythe against the ground, ending my time in the courtyard for the day.

# CHAPTER 4

# Lorna Sydney

They pulled me from Hala before I had a chance to kiss her farewell. I was so focused on how sharply the Grim lord spoke to me, I didn't take the time to comfort my sister. Nether knows when I'll see her face again.

The only comfort I have is knowing she will not have to endure the savagery of that Scullard lover, Purcival, and his minions. No doubt he would have violated my sister and passed her around to all the low-life Scullards in his stead.

If nothing else, the harem of the high court is well thought of. Everyone knows the Prince of Purgia is fair to those who are loyal, and I've only ever seen his harem with such broad smiles, they could brighten the night sky.

Thankfully, still, Hala has at least five watches of the night before she'd have to be with a man. Hopefully by that time, I can instruct her on what to expect.

Thinking of Hala is all I can do as I follow the Grim lord and his guards down a long, narrow hallway. I pass a small group of feather-clad females and a few male-kind smoking lotus flowers as they lay on large pillows in a room that looks like a small garden.

"Sabine! Throw it to me!" one scorpion-tailed woman shouts as they bounce a glass ball around. *Sabine.* I look to the side, where I see a woman with three breasts, adorned in red, seated on a large slab of stone. There's a lotus flower between her fingers as she waves at the Grim lord when he passes by.

"I'll call for you soon, my sweet!" he says over his shoulder without looking at her.

She only chuckles in reply, but her envious gaze stays fixed on me.

We arrive at a large set of black iron double doors, and a guard pushes them open, standing to the side so the Grim lord enters first. I remain at the threshold, unsure what to do.

As he spins on his heel, the Grim lord's face is like a black hole, and I can hardly make out his green eyes.

"Well, are you just going to stand there?" he grouses, waving his guards away.

With a small nod, I look over my shoulder, only to see a sly smile on Dane's face as he closes the door behind me just as I step inside.

Standing in the center of the room, I watch as the Grim lord saunters around, flicking candles with the snap of his hand. He mumbles incoherently as he does, and I take the moment to look around.

His suite is large, bigger than I thought it would be. I am shocked, however, at how dusty and riddled with cobwebs it is. I suppose it doesn't bother a fleshless soul like him, but I feel my skin crawling beneath my cloak.

Still grumbling, he removes layers of his clothing—I hadn't realized he had on more than one gown. Watching him, I see the black snakes slither around his ankles, retreating again up his leg. My eyes remain trained on his legs, but as he peels layers of heavy cloaks from around him, I watch in awe as flesh magically covers bone.

Clawing my hands at my mouth, I'm nervous my gasp alerts him to the prickly fear racing up my spine, but he pays me no mind. Instead, he continues, removing layer after layer until he's left with nothing but his own nakedness.

I'm thankful my hooded nature conceals my eyes, lest they betray me as I ogle him from across the room. I do what I can to keep my composure. Whatever remains of the skeleton demon that haunts the minds of mortals and otherworldly alike is gone; what stands before me now is a dangerously beautiful naked man.

His hair is sleek and black like a raven, skin pale as a shadow moon, and his glorious green eyes pierce into my own like he's digging for secrets tucked beneath my bone. Half of his calavera-painted face remains ominous and dark, while the other half reveals youthful features accompanied by hardened lines of maturity.

*He is gorgeous!*

I watch as the snakes tether to his skin like tattoos, his pale skin marked from head to toe in serpents and ancient writings. A large, chiseled chest, with muscular biceps bulging from his arms, are first in my view, but when my eyes trail to his waist, the thick, veiny monster between his legs steals my focus.

I've never seen anything so perfect. I want to touch it, to feel how it moves. *Inside me.*

*Get a hold of yourself, Syd!*

I bite my lip; here I am, in his bedchamber, and he's already naked. He doesn't waste any time. I suppose the rumors about him are true. He *is* a sex-crazed demon of death.

"Well," he begins dryly as the stitch painting of his lips curl in such a seductive manner, I feel wetness gather between my thighs. "I suppose it's time."

"Yes, my lord," I answer, unbuttoning my corset.

He licks his lips, folding his arms across his chest as my breasts spill out. I pull my bodice down to my waist, too fearful to let it fall to my feet. It's been a while since I've known a man in this manner, but if this is what it takes to keep Hala safe, so be it.

I watch as his now-hardened member, swinging between his tree trunk-like thighs, flicks upward, aiming for me. He gives it a gentle stroke, groaning as flames dance behind his eyes.

"Damn. You are a sight," he says, examining me. "Tell me," he begins, closing the distance between us, still stroking his hard length. "What sweet offering shall you render to pardon your soul?"

He's so close now, I can feel his breath on my skin. My breasts are pressed against his chest as he trails his hand along my torso, and I try not to moan, fearful his fingers will find their way to my sex. Alas, a small whimper betrays me, and his dark gaze gleams with delight.

"Tell me!" he demands as my eyes roll to the back of my head. I want him to touch me so badly, it hurts.

"I'll offer whatever pleases you, my lord," I confess, knowing that while I'll gladly offer my body for Hala, a part of me wants to do this for reasons beyond my control.

"Mmm..." he groans against my hood. "So you've come to do whatever I want?" His rough hand winds around my waist, tempting my resolve. I feel my nipples harden, and I fear what could come next.

"Hala!" I cry, trying to ward off the burning arousal stirring within me. "I came for Hala!"

He pulls me close, so close that his manhood is bucking between my thighs. "You may have come for Hala, but soon, you will come for me."

She's still trying to catch her breath as her knees buckle. She leans against the cold wall, pulling away from me, but I don't want to let her go. Still, I know if I hold her any longer, there'll be no stopping what comes next.

I've never seen anything or anyone so perfect. Her body calls to me in ways beyond reason—I want to ruin her, make my home in the sweet cavern between her legs, and ruin her some more. I want to throw her down on my bed and shove myself so far inside her, nothing but darkness prevails.

But I cannot.

I need to know more about her, like how and why she has a Grim ring. Even more, I need her to give it to me.

Although I still can't see her face in full, I'm entranced by not only her voluptuous form, but her stubbornness. It doesn't take a genius to know she's doing all she can not to fold so easily, but just as I can barely keep my manhood from seeking his prey, I'm certain if I were to touch it, nothing could keep her sweet spot from leaking all her secrets.

"My lord, please. I'll do whatever you please as long as Hala is kept safe," she repeats quietly against the wall. As she wraps her arms around herself, I can see she feels too exposed in front of me, but I'm not ready for her to cover up just yet.

"Lower your hands to your side," I command, ensuring she hears the authority in my voice.

Sucking in a breath, she restrains her tears, doing as I instruct, and I'm once more rewarded with the sight of her large breasts and the delightful shadow of her curves against the wall.

"When you are in my bedchamber, I want to see you just like this. Do you understand?"

"Yes, my lord, but I cannot remove my hood. It is against—"

Lifting my hand, I quiet her protest. "This will do," I answer harshly, walking toward the seat at the end of my bed. "When we are in my chambers, it is just us two. You are here to serve my needs. Do you understand?"

She dips her head. "Yes, my lord."

Slowly, she begins to pull down her bodice, but I issue a grunt of warning. "It's best if you keep some things private." I nearly choke on the words.

"My lord? But I thought you said–"

"If I catch even an eyeful of that pretty little thing between your legs, I will fuck you into oblivion. Do you understand?"

Her breath hitches, and she bites her bottom lip. "Yes?" It's more of a question, as though she wonders why I wouldn't want to do just that.

Her hands once more find their way to cover her breasts, only for her to drop them to her side.

"Are you shy of your nakedness?" She only shrugs in response. "Were you violated?"

Her shoulders square. "No, my lord, but Hala–"

Ugh. Again with the sister. I'll let it slide for now, but I can't hear of her every day. "What about her?" I turn away to hide my irritation; this constant discussion of her sister is enough to control the beast between my legs.

"Nothing–nothing. I misspoke."

I don't have to see her eyes to know she is lying. She's likely still worried about the girl falling to the Prince's harem when she comes of age. Little does she know, the Prince hardly touches his harem. Sure, they parade before him or bathe him from time to time, but he never so much as gives them a singular thought. Hala is far safer in the high court of the Prince than she is anywhere else, but I can't tell her that. Nor can I tell her that Prince Kharon is in the earth realm.

I need her to get comfortable here. That's the only way I'll make her feel safe enough to tell me about the Grim ring. Sex could be one way, but for some reason, I want better for her than that.

I just can't let her know it yet.

"Very well then," I say, patting my knees and standing from my seat. "I suppose we should get to the business of the bedchamber."

"Oh," she exclaims, and the way her pouty lips form an *O* makes me want to fuck that pretty little mouth until she's dripping with the darkness of me down her chin.

I wave her toward me. "Come here."

"Yes, my lord." She does as I instruct, taking small steps toward me as her bountiful bosom leads the way.

She gathers her hands at her waist, her breasts pressing together, forming a heart shape pattern, and it's all the signal I need to know this woman was handpicked just for me. It's a strange feeling, to want someone I've only just met so badly, but I want this woman.

Still, I work hard to force aside the gnawing, desirous craving I have for her. There's still too much about her I don't know.

"Now, tell me about yourself. Your name, Lorna-Sydney, is that what you'd prefer to be called?"

"Syd is fine, my lord. Lorna was my mother's name. My own is Sydney."

*Sydney.* I repeat her name, and I like the way it sounds on my tongue. Even more, I like watching the way her mouth moves when she says it. I can tell she's not one to smile often, but her pouty little lips curve ever so slightly as she utters her own name.

"Very well, then," I answer, working hard to keep my eyes off her breasts. Folding one leg over my knee, I hope to distract my dick a little. "Now, tell me what brings a woman like you to beg for my aide. I am no simpleton. What is it that you really want from me?"

Syd shrugs her shoulders, shaking her head. "My lord, it's only a few night watches until Festivus. Everyone in Purgia seeks to gain your favor or that of the Prince."

With one arm now across my waist as my fingers scratch my chin, I give her a once over. I'm not buying it. "Sure, many would rather be consumed by my mirth than be relegated to Hades. That is common knowledge. You want something else. Tell me!" I demand, slightly impressed with how she remains cool despite my tone.

"I don't know what you mean, my lord," she insists, turning her head slightly.

Jumping up from my seat, I make my way in front of her. "Syd, tell me the truth." My hand is on her chin, and I lift her face until I can see just beyond the bridge of her nose. I'd hoped to catch a glimpse of her eyes, but I don't see anything. "Now!" I squeeze her cheeks between my hands. "And don't tell me it's for Hala!"

"But it is, my lord!" she counters, gritting out her words through clenched teeth. Her back arches, and she rises to the balls of her feet as I lift her chin higher, forcing her to press her breasts into my chest. My manhood instantly responds, springing upward and hitting her in the abdomen when I feel a twinge of wetness on my chest.

I look down and see a shimmering milky substance gathered between us.

Syd gasps as I drop my hand from her face. "Oh! I'm so sorry, sire." She backs away, palming her breasts in embarrassment.

Taking both her wrists in my grip, I pull her hands down to her sides. "Let me take a look at you," I groan as Syd shyly leans her chin to her shoulder. She is a lovely sight! I watch as tiny drops like diamonds leak from her nipples and run down her waist. In all my Nether years, I've never seen anyone so enchanting. "You are quite fetching," I whisper, still admiring her beauty.

Her shoulders slump some, and I know she's more than humiliated, but I don't want her to feel an ounce of shyness in front of me. I want her to feel free, but I don't know how to make her comfortable. At least not yet.

Slowly lifting her chin, Syd turns her face back toward me. "This is why I came to you, my lord," she painfully admits, faint black tears falling to her chin.

Here goes nothing. Time for me to bare it all before the Grim lord. This wasn't how I thought it would go, but here we are. My mind spins as the right words fail to form in my mouth, and I'm thankful he can't see the confused look in my eyes.

"You better start talking." He squeezes my wrist, pulling me close.

"Purcival!" I blurt out, and his eyes narrow so sharply, I think arrows will strike me dead.

"What?" he snaps.

"The LowLand magistrate, my lord," I continue.

He quickly releases me from his grip. "I know who he is—tell me why you're spitting another man's name in my face!"

I try to ignore the drip of jealousy in his voice as I continue. "Yes, my lord. Purcival has plans to use my sister Hala as a milking wench for his wretched Scullards."

He backs away from me, frowning in confusion. Turning around, he goes back to his chair and plops down. "And why should I care about such plans? I've already redeemed your sister from such a fate."

"You asked me why I begged for your aid. That is why. To protect Hala. If I thought I could simply barter my own body for her before Purcival, I would—"

A cold wind rushes through the room, and suddenly, I'm pinned against the wall. Before I can mutter my next words, I once more feel the Grim lord's hand on me, this time on my throat as he holds me tight. "You won't dare offer what is mine to that wretch! You are mine! Is that clear?"

My eyes pop in surprise as my breath splinters within his grip. "Yes, my lord," I manage to squeak out.

Slowly, the Grim lord relaxes his grip, but he keeps himself firmly pressed against me. "That's my good girl," he breathes at my neck.

"There is no need to worry, my lord," I quietly agree, watchful of the pained glare of his now-darkened eyes. "Besides, Purcival didn't want me. Only the purest, like Hala, can nourish the Scullard Dogs at Purcival's command. I am already sullied, I'm afraid. I'll likely be of no use to you either, sire," I mumble the last part.

My heart sinks knowing that someone like me will never have true love —at least, not in my Specter state. The last time I thought I found a companion, I drove him to madness. Since that day, I vowed never to reveal myself again.

"I'll be the judge of that," he says, softer than I expected, backing away from me. "At any rate, Purcival is a fool. Your breasts look nourishing enough," he adds with a lick of his lips.

"I'm afraid this only happens when I am–um, I hate to say, but when I am—"

"Aroused?" he answers flatly, and I nod in agreement. "Well, girl, that's not some dirty thing to be ashamed of." Pausing for a moment as he leans back in the chair with his arms folded across his chest, he continues examining me from head to toe. As if he could sense himself becoming entranced, he shifts in his seat, plucking his fingers. "Is that it? Is that why you begged for my aid?"

"I feared for our safety, my lord. I mean, it's bad enough that he wanted to use my sister in such a manner, but after he tricked our father by trading his lottery for a seat on the black ships of Hades–"

Now I've got his attention.

Leaning in a bit, the Grim lord lifts a finger toward me. This time, however, I see the black snakes coiling around his wrists as his green eyes brighten in the darkened space. "What did you just say?"

"Purcival tricked our father?" I repeat slowly.

"How so?"

"Have you not heard of what's happening in the LowLands? How the lower court magistrates trick many of the unfortunate souls, like my father, into trading their lottery for a supposed better gain?"

The Grim lord's eyes narrow, and I hear the snakes on his skin hiss in my direction. This time, his face darkens like a hollow tree. "What do you mean a trade? The lottery is solely managed by me." His tone is hard, and the calavera side of his mouth tightens into a thin line.

"Do you not know what's going on out there, my lord? Have you even bothered to look? The people of your province suffer needlessly. The poor, like me and other Specter-folk, or any other Netherfolk long forgotten, are left to the duplicity of the magistrates while you—"

He jumps up from his seat. "While I what?" The snakes hiss louder, and this time, I think it's meant for me. "Mind your next words, girl!"

"I'm sorry, my lord, but you asked for the truth!"

Scoffing, he swipes a dismissive hand through the air. "You dare insinuate treachery, as though the sweet shape of you alone is enough to thwart the Prince's ire if you are found lying?"

"My lord Grim, I have no reason to lie to either you or the Great Prince." I pause, watchful of the snakes lifting from his skin, aimed in my direction. I take special notice, despite whatever anger he has for me, that his manhood remains pointed at me as he grips his length. Still, I try not to let it distract me. "I came to you in truth."

"Did you?" he turns his head slightly. "And what of this?" He uses his free hand to reach between my breasts, yanking at my father's heirloom.

I pull away from him, tearing the cord from his hands. As I do, our fingers graze, and a wave of static shock ripples between us. We share a gasp, our gaze locked with one another.

The world spins around us, as if time stands still. The room inverts into a diamond-like pattern as vertigo sets in, and a dizzying haze overtakes me. Although I know it's impossible, I swear I see his face in full—no calavera, no paintings of a sugared skull, as the mortals call it. No, it's just his perfection; smooth skin, bronzed by nightshade, sculpted in shadow as the light of the moon reveals the calm storm brewing behind his eyes.

His touch was magnetic; I've never felt anything like that before, and oh, do I want to feel it again.

Back when I shared my bed with Grigori, there was nothing electric or night shattering. I mean, it was nice for what it was, but nothing remotely close to the feel of the Grim lord's skin upon my own.

Even when I disclosed Purcival's intent to have my sister lined up to be milked by his mangy Scullards, my mind only thought of the desirous gaze in his eyes and how I wished the Grim lord would relieve the ache in my own breasts.

I've never been like this around a man. So needy. So eager. So ridiculously wet. *So soon.*

I thought I could restrain myself—be my normal, cold-hearted Specter self—but here I am, thankful his touch didn't electrocute me, considering how wet I am.

"It was my father's," I confess softly, backing up to create a little more distance between us.

I'm surprised when the Grim lord says nothing. Instead, he just stares at me, speechless, but still holding his shaft. I can't believe he's been naked this entire time.

"Interesting," he mumbles, licking his lips before turning away from me once more. "Well, enough small talk. It's time."

"Time for what, my lord?" I ask, and my needy sex nearly spasms at the thought of what comes next.

"To learn how to care for this bedchamber."

My heart sinks a little; I don't know why I thought this was going somewhere else. "What?" I blurt out. His brows crease, and I realize I said it out loud.

A dark grin hovers at the corner of his mouth. "Why yes, that's actually what I was going to say before you distracted me with these sweet peaks." He points two fingers at my chest. "Not to mention your little sob story about Purcival."

"Sob story?" I bite back. I can hardly breathe. I feel the room spinning again, but not for the same reasons. "But you–you took off your clothes. So naturally, I thought—"

"That I wanted to *fuck* you?" The Grim lord intentionally hits the *F* hard, and he lets out a dark chuckle that reverberates around the room. "Please, darling, if I wanted to bury myself in that sweet little nighthole of yours, I would have done so by now."

Now my heart is out of my chest.

I've made a fool of myself.

Sauntering to a small door on the other side of his room, he opens it. "This is the closet. Come see." He waves me to his side, and I find a dripping ceiling with a dingy bucket, a broom, and a few sponges. "Everything you need for cleaning and keeping my chambers up to par is in here."

"Yes, sire." I almost hate hearing the sullen sound of my voice. While this is what I practically begged him for, I thought perhaps this could be something–I don't know–*something more.*

But those were just the thoughts of a desperate woman who hasn't had her fill in ages. I thought running to the Grim lord was the best idea. Father spoke so well of him, but the Grim lord's behavior is as erratic as they come. I think Father only idolized him from afar. Perhaps he thought anything was better than a low court magistrate like Purcival.

"Good girl," he grins, grazing his knuckles softly across my chin. "Be sure to clean in here well. This is where you'll take your rest, after all." He walks off to a murky corner and grabs something that looks like a towel, but I can't make it out.

"What do you mean this is where I'll sleep? There's hardly room to—"

"Well, you didn't think you'd be lying with me, did you?" His shoulders roll in amusement. "What a foolish idea!" The Grim lord steps out from the shadows. "Besides, one thing you ought to know is that I rest alone. My bed is made for a very singular use: me."

Now I know he's lying. There's no way no one else ever gets in his bed.

"I don't have to see your eyes to know what you're thinking, love. So before you trouble your pretty little Specter brain any further, I'll let you in on a little secret: I've never fucked anyone in my bed. Some things are sacred."

With that, he ambles to a side wall, where I hear what sounds like rain.

"I'm going to wash." He waves the towel over his shoulder. "Start cleaning the closet and the rest of the chamber for now. I'll show you how to clean me later."

I couldn't get away from her fast enough.

What in the hell was I thinking, bringing that woman to my chambers?

I don't know who's to blame: the ache between my legs, or my role as Grim.

Sure, I'd like nothing more than to fuck her into oblivion. Then again, I'd do almost anything to take that Grim ring from between her bosom. Adding another Grim ring to my arsenal could not only give me more power over the lands of Mirth, but a means to reclaim the lands of my people from Hades himself.

Nether knows I'd do anything to restore the full power of the Grim to my people. Procuring that ring could be just what I need to make that a reality.

Who am I kidding? Right now, I don't give a damn about a ring. All I can think about is her.

That's why I've got one arm propped against the stone wall while my other hand strokes the gnawing need from my manhood. It's taking everything inside me not to run out from under this shower, throw her on my bed, and grind into her until only my name is on her lips. But she deserves better than what I can give.

I'll just have to wait until she wants me the way I want her. Right now, however, her only focus is her sister. While I'm sure she'd take her pounding like a good girl, I know she'd only do so for Hala.

Since the best gifts are those most eagerly awaited, I'll wait however long it takes until she *wants* to give it to me. For now, I'll just have to use the dark musings of my own mind.

I think of Syd's luscious curves, of the sweet honey exuding from her breasts, and even the way her shadows cast her in perfection as the candle-light illuminates her frame.

She is breathtaking!

*Harder. Faster.*

I keep stroking until I feel what I only can make out to be the makings of joy bubbling within me. I've never felt anything quite like this before, and I doubt I ever will again.

Usually, I only climax to quiet the need between my legs. I've never known anything like this before.

The way I want to drive my steel length between her perfect, perky peaks, allowing her sweet milk to drench me, only to watch her suck it off as I fuck her pretty little mouth...

That's where my mind goes.

What is happening to me?

My stomach knots in my bowels, and a jittery sensation claws over my body as I wrangle the monster between my thighs until I'm spraying the walls with everything I've got.

"Sydney!" Her name rips through my clenched jaws as I draw out the last drop. One more yelp and I'm panting, out of breath as I lean against the shower wall. Heaving in hard breaths, I try to compose myself, to think of anything to relieve myself of her haunting presence.

"My lord Grim?" I hear her small voice echo through my bathing chamber.

Startled, I press beneath the waterfall, hopeful she doesn't see the mess I've made in her honor. "What is it?" I growl, quickly lathering the yucca root over my body.

"I thought I heard my name, my lord," she answers softly.

Turning my face upward into the cascading fountain, I palm my face, needing to blur my view of Syd's voluptuous silhouette standing in the archway.

"Yes—fetch me my towel from the post." I point to the side wall, my free hand still on my face as I try to keep my attention off her.

Syd moves faster than I expect, and I sense her standing closer than before. "Here you go, my lord," she says, stretching the soft fabric toward me.

Dropping my hands to my side, I test my resolve and turn toward her. Even through the steamy haze forming from my shower, she is a treasured sight before my eyes.

Her perky, ripe breasts, glimmering with the misty dew of her leakage from before, make my mouth water. With her head lowered, modestly turned away from me, her back arches just enough to highlight the plump roundness of her tight ass and the sweet spread of her hips beneath her bodice.

Even the gentle way the cape of her hood blows in the breeze flowing from the window accentuates her curves, as though she were a gift from Night itself made just for me. Perhaps she is, but I know too well not to tempt fate.

Taking her wrist, I turn her toward me. I need to see her in full. I also need her to see what she does to me as my partner in crime once more rises to the occasion.

Slowly, Syd's head lifts, and she bites her lower lip as I place her hand on my chest.

"Soon, you'll learn how to clean me. For now, you can dry me off." My speech is ragged, my tongue slack in my jaw as I grit out the words.

"My lord?" she questions.

"Like this," I begin, moving her hand in a circular motion to pat the water off me. Again, her breath hitches, but she takes a deep breath and continues as I lead her hands over my body. Every wanton stroke leaves me breathless, and it's taking everything in me not to pin her against the shower wall.

Rising to the balls of her feet, Syd removes the water from my shoulders and neck. When she moves toward my arms, one of my serpents gnashes its fangs in her direction.

Squealing, she goes to step back, but I pull her close. "Don't be frightened," I groan against her hood. "My familiars are just puttering around with you. They want to charm you, gain your favor."

"Oh," she sighs, her gaze still watchful of the way it coils around my wrist, flicking its forked tongue toward her. "Just puttering, you say?" Syd chuckles, curling her lip into a small smile as she reaches around my waist to wipe the small of my back.

Her hand trails to my thigh, and she slowly drops to her knees. Another serpent near my waist lifts from my skin, as do all the others as we collectively admire the sight of Sydney bowed before me, my largest, most vicious serpent aimed for her mouth.

It would be so easy to slither between her pretty little lips and ram myself down her throat until she choked, black tears swimming down her cheeks. Still, I cannot. She deserves so much better than a wretch like me can offer.

Looking at her dutifully attending to me with a care I've never known makes me want to repent the depraved ways I wish to sully her body for my own filthy pleasure. Still, I am not a repentant man, nor will I relent in committing to memory every wretched thing I want to do with and to her.

She bends over, and her luscious breasts graze my feet as she dries me off, calf-to-foot. My dick hardens at the sight of her, nearly smacking her in the face as she lifts her head toward me.

"Sire," she whispers, her hands outstretched with the towel as she reaches for my length. I wish I knew what she was thinking. Do I repulse her, or is she only thinking of Hala? Perhaps she's still thinking of Purcival. The last thing I want is someone else on her mind when she takes me for the first time. "May I?" she asks sweetly.

I cringe. The thought of her touching me is driving me insane. The thoughts of me touching her in return is driving me batshit mad.

"My lord?" she repeats, her hands ever so slightly hovering around my hard length. I want to punish her for making me want her so badly. I don't know if it's because her breasts squeeze together as her arms reach for me, but the thought of thrusting my manhood between her peaks and into her mouth is a fantasy on replay in my mind.

"Don't, Sydney!" I bark, ripping the towel from her hands and wrapping it around my waist.

Syd sits back on her feet, her lovely bosom bouncing as the shiny heirloom dances between her cleavage, reminding me what I truly brought her here for. The Grim ring. That's why she is here. Nothing more.

"My lord, I'm sorry if I—"

I yank her up from the floor before she can finish. The sight of her still kneeling before me won't do anything to lessen the ache between my legs.

"It's okay, Syd," I say, straightening her hood. "You just don't deserve it yet. Besides, that's one serpent who doesn't putter around. He bites. Hard."

"**I** *don't deserve it yet?*" I mutter to myself as he leads us back to the bedchamber. What in the hell is that supposed to mean?

Spinning hard on his heel, the Grim lord turns back toward me. "That's right, love. Only I decide when and what you deserve. Is that clear?" he snaps, wagging a long finger.

"Yes, my lord," I reply. Although I could've sworn I walked in on the tail-end of him jacking off with my name on his lips, perhaps I got it wrong.

Pointing to a large walnut armoire, he continues, "Now, pass me the first two articles inside."

Opening the double doors, I'm surprised to find his clothes neatly hung, blouse-to-trousers. Strangely, however, I notice how they all look the same. While I'm sure someone of his stature has access to an array of fabrics in the Soleil, I find it curious he chooses to stick with the same ensemble.

I offer him the clothes, and he lays them at the foot of his bed. I suppose he'll expect me to change him next. Swallowing my pride, I step forward, hopeful his snakes don't choose to bite me this time around as I watch them slither through his skin.

Lifting his palm in warning, he motions for me to keep my distance. "That'll be all for now."

"Yes, my lord Grim. I can finish my chores in my dwelling if you don't mind."

He clears his throat. "Actually, I do mind. I need a little privacy. You can step out with Dane to the courtyard."

Once more, he's plucking at his fingers, deliberately avoiding eye contact. I know I'm not much to look at, but he's vexing. One minute, he can't take his eyes off me, and the next, he can't stand the sight of me.

This time, I only offer a slight bow. I don't know what to make of his moods, and I fear I'll say the wrong thing, ruining both mine and Hala's chance at a life beyond Purcival's mangy Scullards.

As I make my way to the door, my hands barely touch the handle when I once more feel a brisk wind prickle at my pores.

The Grim lord's hand is upon my wrist, halting my exit. "Now, now," he croons, leaning into the side of my neck. "It's best you keep what belongs to me private." Pressing himself against me, he pushes my back against the door. Like a feather, his hands glide over my shoulders and down my waist until he reaches my corset. Slowly tugging it up my abdomen, he cups my breasts, gently tucking the pair back into my laced bodice. As he does, his thumb grazes my nipple, instantly causing a small drip. Pinching the sensitive skin between his heavily inked fingers, I wince at both the pleasure and pain.

"That's my good girl," he groans, swirling his fore and middle fingers in his mouth. He moans as his now darkened gaze sets back on me. "Now go. I'd hate for you to leak all over me after I just washed."

My heart nearly croaks at his words; I hate how he makes me long for him one second, only to be repulsed in the next. I don't know what I thought it would be. Then again, it's still a far better fate than watching Hala be passed around like a ragdoll or worse.

The Grim lord is back at his seat, fidgeting again with his fingers before I have a chance to turn the door handle.

Like magic, the door swings open, and I see Dane on the other side. He offers a courtesy nod before bowing at the waist as the Grim lord comes into full view.

"Dane, please show this one around my galley and stir me up something to eat."

"Yes, sire," Dane nods bows again.

Stepping over the threshold, I let out a breath. I hadn't noticed I'd been holding my breath for so long. The air feels crisper, cooler than the stuffiness of his bedchamber.

"Oh, Dane, one more thing: Please send for Sabine."

I stop just beyond the doorpost, looking over my shoulder. The Grim lord's eyes are dancing. He's amused. Either he's toying with my emotions, or the thought of whatever Sabine has to offer has him giddy with delight.

If I didn't need his help, I'd lift my hood, reveal myself, and send him into a fit of madness. Although, with him being a Grim, I'm not certain my power would have the same effect, but it would so be worth the effort.

He is a complete asshole.

"As you wish, my lord," Dane dutifully answers, closing the door.

All I see is a glowing pair of green eyes and a mischievous grin as the oversized door closes.

With a loud clap of his hands, Dane quiets the sound of the harps and other fluted instruments playing in the courtyard that I hadn't noticed before.

Looking around, I now see there are folk with instruments in a small balcony above us, a few more gathered around the woman in red, Sabine, still smoking lotus flowers in the common area.

"Sabine," Dane shouts, adding one more thunderous clap.

She continues laughing, passing the lotus flower back and forth with the scorpion-looking woman. Her bright red eyes bounce quickly to Dane after her gaze rolls past me.

"What?" she barks back dismissively while batting the glass ball to another man in a corner.

"The Grim lord requires your company," Dane huffs as literal smoke shoots through his nostrils.

The man hits the ball toward the scorpion woman, and she offers it back to Sabine. Hissing at the woman, Sabine's long, forked tongue lashes out as she knocks the ball away from her. The woman and the others gathered around Sabine skulk into a dark corner as Sabine steps down from her makeshift throne.

"Fine!" she grouses, fluffing her three-layered cleavage. "I suppose he's kept me waiting long enough." Her tongue rattles between her sharp teeth. As she stands, I notice a thin, pointed tail peeking out from under her georgette gown. She sways her thick black hair to one side, and I spy two pointed horns.

She's a Goldhorn!

I've never seen one before. Creatures like Sabine are thought to originate from the ibex, the most sensual of horned beasts in the Netherworld. No wonder the Grim lord has her at his beck and call. I'm sure someone of her stead is capable of matching his stamina.

"Chelamma!" Sabine says over her shoulder as she saunters past me and Dane. "Come. I'm sure our lord Grim would rather play with two," she continues, sashaying down the dark hall.

The scorpion woman, Chelamma, jumps up from the corner, quickly scaling the wall and floor to make her way to Sabine's side.

"He only asked for–" Dane begins, but he is instantly quieted by the raise of Sabine's hand.

Still slithering forward, Sabine shoots a look at me over her shoulder before casting a dark grin at Dane. "I think I know what my lord Grim needs most." She offers a quick wink before opening the door to the Grim lord's chambers as she and Chelamma enter.

"Sabine, my dulcet darling." The Grim lord's hearty tone echoes through the halls of his hallowed chambers.

My stomach turns as the door closes behind Sabine and Chelamma. Hearing how happy he is to see them confuses me. I've only spent a short while with him, and yet I find the makings of envy clawing up my spine.

This is not an emotion I'm accustomed to, nor is it an emotion I wish to endure.

Instead, I suck in a breath, square my shoulders, and hold my head high. I did not agree to be his concubine. If all he wants from me is to keep his bedchamber, so be it. I have no interest in sharing myself with anyone who doesn't want me—much less wants to get to know me. I've humiliated myself enough for the Grim lord, but that ends now.

Even if I have to repeat it like a mantra every day for the rest of my life, I will do so as long as I always remember the reason I'm here.

I'm doing this for Hala.

For more night watches than I can recall, this has been our habit. Sabine. Naked. In my chambers.

Yet, instead of fulfilling my desires, although I get great pleasure from this vantage point, I watch, in my seat, as she and her newest trinket, Chelamma, deliver bouts of passion, blow after blow, until they've had their fill.

Sabine may be a spirited Goldhorn for her species, but from the moment I met her, I knew anatomically, there was nothing I could offer her. For any other man, it would be a blow to his ego, but not for me. I have no interest in being with anyone who has no interest in me.

We do, however, have a mutual understanding.

She serves as my chamber consort and lead of my harem, leaving her brethren to believe she is fulfilling her duties as a Goldhorn while unsuspectingly luring young maidens to my lair to enter my mirth. Nethers knows I need my fill more than what Festivus allows.

Since Goldhorns are bred for their sexual prowess in the beds of royals, it is the expectation of her folk that she is here to exclusively meet my needs. We maintain the pretense. It works for both of us.

I don't have to wait until Festivus to fill the void of my mirth, and Sabine can fulfill her needs without her folk ever being the wiser. Sure, I still get off from watching, and I often give instructions to ensure I stroke off my need, but that's about how far it goes.

In fact, that's how it's been going for quite some time.

Chelamma is squirming on the hammock, her hands tied above her head as Sabine feasts on her sex. She's nearing her climax as Sabine continues her ruthless assault, causing Chelamma to quiver beneath her grip. The pair moan as their shared pleasure combusts, echoing through my chamber in a sound I'm sure can be heard throughout Purgia—a sound I'm sure everyone thinks I'm responsible for.

Normally, the sight of the two women alone would send me into a fit of my own, but not this time. There's only one woman on my mind: Sydney.

Knowing I sent her away without her ever knowing how I feel for her crushes me more than I can ever admit. The look on her face when I called for Sabine while sending her away makes me wonder if, perhaps, she was beginning to think of more than her sister Hala.

Who am I kidding? She is likely more upset that she must dwell with me when she'd rather be with her sister.

"Would you like a taste, my lord Grim?" Sabine moans, throwing her hair over her shoulder as she looks at me. She parts Chelamma's legs, but I turn my head before I see anything more. Besides, I've seen it before, and I'm not interested.

Swiping my hand through the air, I turn toward the window, peering outside just beyond the River Styx. It's a beautiful sight this time of night.

Thankfully, Sabine gets the drift. My nonresponse tells her all she needs to know.

The hammock sways a bit as she and Chelamma hop down onto the floor. "I'll be out in a moment," Sabine says, and I hear her give Chelamma a kiss. My door opens and closes quickly, but I know Sabine is still here. "So, would my lord Grim like to tell me what's bothering him? Or would he like me to guess?" She adds a small chuckle as she saunters to the side of the window, careful not to block my view.

I dart a brief glance her way, thankful she's now covered in her robe. A grunt is all I offer in return, and she folds her arms, smiling as she leans against the wall.

"My, my, my," she begins, shaking her head as her shoulders roll in amusement. "I never thought I'd see the day."

Rolling my eyes, I huff, popping up from my seat as I find the clothes Sydney left for me on the corner of bed and begin to dress.

"I don't know what it is you think you see, but I'm more than certain you are wrong," I grumble.

Still shaking her head, Sabine wags a pointed finger. "I doubt it, my lord. Then again, I've never seen you so wound up over a woman in all our time together. She must be a rare find indeed! Hmm... I wonder," she says, locking her knuckles beneath her chin.

"What?" I say, buttoning my top.

"Well, she's a Specter, is she not?"

I shrug my shoulders. "Yeah, so?"

"It's just...it's been quite a spell since we've shared, and seeing as I've never had a Specter before, perhaps we could—"

Nothing but madness clouds my view as my grimly shadows carry me in front of Sabine in an instant, my hand clawing her throat. Two serpents from either side of my arm slither out from under my sleeve, gnashing toward Sabine. Struggling to breathe, Sabine's eyes bulge as she feigns a weak smile.

"I-I'm sorry, my lord," she manages a breath.

I'm still gripping her throat as a low snarl bellows through me, the form of my hollowed darkness beginning to take root.

"Please, my—my lord," Sabine continues, her widened eyes gawking at me as she sees her own demise mirrored in the horridness of my being.

Looking into her eyes, I see me. A black abyss rests where my eyes and mouth should be. Bone, ghastly with withered skin, etches the outline of my face, leaving nothing but the remnant of a skeletal creature in her view.

It's not often that this side of me comes out to play in my chambers, but the thought of anyone touching Sydney, even Sabine, who I'm used to sharing partners with, is driving me to the brink of madness.

Slowly releasing her, I feel my fleshly form take shape as the tethering of my face molds over bone. Sabine's eyes are still gaped as she fearfully watches me, careful of my fingers trailing the base of her jugular.

"Sydney is mine," I grit through clenched teeth, still awaiting the last part of my skin to fold over my mouth.

"Yes, my lord Grim," Sabine mutters, catching her breath while clawing at her own neck.

As my familiars once more twine themselves back into my skin, I turn away from Sabine, doing what I can to regain my composure.

Letting out a weak laugh, Sabine rakes her hands through her hair, shrugging her shoulders. "Well, see? I was right." She feigns another laugh. She refuses to let herself look weak, even in front of me. It's an impressive front, but her wary eyes tell the truth. "I knew that girl had you spun."

A grunt is all I offer in return, choosing to let Sabine think whatever she wants. I owe her no explanation, nor do I have the words to craft such a response.

"Just promise me one thing," she adds, sliding her foot back into her sandals. I only tilt my head, letting her know I'll hear it. "Whatever becomes of you two, please keep a place for me in your court. I'd hate to be disavowed by my brethren for losing my position as your royal consort. If I thought the Reaper lord would–"

I lift my hand in protest, silencing her. "You have nothing to fear, my dear Sabine. Of all things, I am a keeper of my word."

She offers a small bow, and I take special notice of the tears hovering in the corner of her eyes.

Taking a deep breath, I make my way to her. Careful to ensure my movements are as non-threatening as possible, I slowly reach for her shoulder. Sabine's watchful gaze stays fixed on my hands while glancing at my face, and I know she's afraid I'll return to my ghastly form.

"You will always have a place in my court, dear one." I want to tell her how Sydney has my world spinning on its axis and something thumping in the dark hole where no heart resides, but I keep those thoughts to myself.

Still, Sabine's eyes dance as she looks at me, as I'm sure my expression is giving everything away. "Thank you, my lord," Sabine says sweetly. Gently taking my hand from her shoulder and kissing my knuckles, she offers another curtsy before exiting my chamber.

I lean against the closed door as my eyes drift around my room. I never noticed how quiet it feels. Lonely. I've never felt lonely before now, and I know it's not because Sabine left.

It's Sydney.

Her presence alone filled these hallowed halls with something I never knew I needed. So, I'll sit here, waiting patiently, until she returns.

# CHAPTER 10

# Lorna Sydney

"You're adding too much saffron!" Dane snips over my shoulder as I stir the stew.

Huffing, I roll my eyes. "Where do you think the saffron comes from?" I mumble under my breath.

Stepping to my side, Dane quirks a singular brow, his tusks quivering at the delicious smell of the stew. "Really?"

I grab another spoon and dip it into the pot. "Here, try some," I say, offering him a taste. Hesitant, he looks at me and back to the spoon a few times before deciding to try it. His mouth rolls into a gentle smile as he stares up at me.

"Like it?" I ask as he shakes his head in agreement. I smile. "I made this for my father all the time." The thought makes my eyes water.

"You did?" Dane questions, leaning back against the wall, folding his arms over his chest. I nod, adding a pinch of pepper. "Interesting," he groans, twisting his mouth to one side.

"How so?"

He scratches his lofty beard. "Well, I always thought this was just a favorite meal of death dealers like Grim and Reaper. I don't know many others who enjoy it. I mean, I've come to like it, since I make it quite often for the Grim lord."

I shrug my shoulders. "All I know is that my father loved it. He said my mother made it for him all the time. He taught me her recipe." I catch a quick tear with the back of my hand. Thankfully, Dane seems to be distracted by something outside of the kitchen.

"What in the hell–" Dane barks, shoving a cart of wild mushrooms out of his way.

I turn around, peering around his shoulder as I see a bunch of folk gathered just outside. There's shouting and grumbling, more raised voices and the sound of someone getting knocked into something that crashes like glass.

"Stay here," he frowns, drawing out his club-stick. "Let me see what's going on."

He doesn't give me a chance to reply before marching off through the archway. I continue stirring the pot, thinking of my father and Hala, how I miss them so much. More tears fall from my face and into the pot, and there's a sizzling noise as the stew bubbles. Nervously, I stir in more crocus leaves while turning down the heat, hopeful to settle the pot.

"Get over here!" I hear Dane shout behind me. I turn quickly, fearful he thinks I've poisoned the soup. I'm thankful, however, to see him holding a gorgon with his arms behind his back. "Keep still!" he fusses, tightening his hold. "Look, I'll be right back. I need to take this one to lock up. You stay here, and I'll come back for you," he says gruffly.

"I'll be right here." I nod toward the pot. "It'll be a little while before it's ready."

"Very well then," Dane huffs, shoving the gorgon in the back toward the door. "Just don't add any more saffron." He manages a slight smile before heading back out.

Pulling a small wooden chair to the stove, I take a seat. I thumb through a dusty recipe book from the counter, wondering who it belongs to. Staring around the galley, I decide to busy myself with cleaning. If I'll be primarily responsible for the care of the Grim lord, I probably should work on organizing things to my liking. It's pretty evident no one has given it any thought.

I spend most of my time sweeping, dusting,, and wiping down all the hard surfaces. I can't believe no one has thought to keep this part of the royal court clean. Who knows? Maybe the Grim lord likes his things messy, or maybe he truly chose me because he needed someone to bring some order to the chaos. Whatever the case, I'm certainly the woman for the job. I can't function in mess!

I chuckle at the thought. Father always said I leave things better than how I found them. I suppose that's true even now.

The smell of the stew hits my nose, and I set the broom to the side to give the pot one final stir before turning the heat down to simmer. I slice a few pieces of oat bark and place them on the serving tray. I'm not sure if he'll like it with his stew, but since it's here in the kitchen, I'll assume he does.

Just as I'm finishing the garnishments to the tray, I hear a small yet familiar whimpering sound. I wonder if perhaps Dane left someone injured from the ruckus. Wiping my hands on the apron Dane gave me, I step to the archway and look around.

While I don't immediately see anyone, I hear the small cries once more. Circling my gaze around a wooden trough, I'm surprised to see Hala and another small girl curled up in the corner.

"Hala!" I shriek in shock.

"She wouldn't stop crying," the small girl says, her arms around my sister's waist.

"Syd!" Hala cries with her arms outstretched. "I thought I'd never see you again."

I kneel at her side. "What are you doing here?"

"She told us to hide," the small girl says. Her face is bright, like a dusty rose, with big golden eyes and shimmering hair.

"Who?" I ask, gently pulling Hala to my side and out of the girl's hold.

"Pella," the girl answers with a sweet smile. "The Viridian Sprite."

I nod as I carefully give my sister a once over.

The small girl pats my shoulder. "She is not harmed, but Pella said she saw Scullard scouts on patrol nearby. She said she would light the way when it's safe to return to the meeting post." The girl holds up a seeing stone. They're used as trackers; if someone wants you to find them, they'll ignite a flame only the holder of the stone can see.

"Who are you?" I question.

"I am Liv, a fairy of Kilgo Falls. Pella, ward of the Great Prince, is my friend. I was with her when the Scullards were spotted," she explains.

My heart plummets as I wonder if Purcival sent them to look for me and Hala. We haven't been here a full watch of the night, and we're already being tracked!

"I'm just so happy to see you, Syd," Hala says, squeezing my waist.

I grab her face, examining her round cheeks puffing out from beneath her hood. "And I you, my sister," I begin, kissing the top of her head and pulling her into my embrace. "Thank you, Liv," I smile, appreciative of her keeping my sister safe.

Liv's golden eyes grow bright as she looks at the stone in her hand. "It's time," she says, nodding at the stone.

"No!" Hala squeals, squeezing me tighter. "I can't leave you, Syd. Not a second time!"

Taking her chin in my hand, I wipe the two black tears that have fallen to her chin. "Be strong, my sister. Remember, you said–"

"No, Syd!" she protests, her grip tight on my arms. "I thought I could be strong without you. I can't! I can't!" She continues her tearful plea and buries her face in my chest.

"We have to get going," Liv says, standing up. "Before the light grows dim. Who knows how long we'll have until the Scullards reappear."

"Please, Syd!" Hala whines with a strong hold on my waist as I bring us to our feet.

I look around the galley. I don't see Dane, or anyone for that matter. "What if I took you halfway?" I say, peering around both Liv and Hala.

Liv takes Hala's hands. "How does that sound, Hala? You'll have both me and your sister."

"All the way," Hala counters, poking out her bottom lip. There's the stubborn little sister I've grown to love.

"Half. And we're losing time." I keep my tone flat; she needs to know this is the deal.

Drawing her mouth into a thin line, Hala nods, knowing I won't budge.

"We should get going," Liv says with a gentle squeeze to my sister's hand and a wink at me. "It's not that far."

I look over my shoulder and into the kitchen. The stew is turned down low and should be fine until I return. Hopefully, I'll be back before Dane or anyone else sees me.

~

Liv leads us along through a darkened cavern adjacent to the Grim lord's courtyard. While I'm thankful no one sees us, there's a gnawing feeling in my gut that I'll regret leaving my post.

"So," Hala says over shoulder after too many moments of silent stubbornness pass. "How's the Grim lord? Is he nice?"

Thinking of his vacillating personality only annoys me. "He's true to his word." It's all I can say so as not to trouble her further. "But at least I get to make a steaming pot of crocus stew!" I exclaim, giving my sister a gentle shove.

"Mmm..." Hala moans with a small chuckle. "I thought I smelled something good. I could surely use some."

"We're here," Liv announces, turning at the end of the cavern where I hear more folk walking by. "Pella will be just on the other side of the fountain."

I share a smile with Liv. "Thank you for keeping an eye on my sister, Liv. It was nice meeting you."

"The pleasure was all mine," she says with a graceful bow as she exits the cavern.

Hala throws her arms around my waist. "I love you so much, Syd!"

"I love you too, Hala." I hug her hard, and as much as I don't want to let her go, I do. I didn't get to hug her the first time, and I'm just thankful to get this opportunity.

Surprisingly, Hala breaks from our embrace first and rushes out of the cavern. My heart plummets to the pit of my stomach as I watch her walk away, but I force a smile, knowing she is safe.

~

Rushing out of the cavern, I barely get a chance to look around when I'm yanked hard from the side.

"Where in the hell have you been?" Dane barks, his singular eye examining me hard.

"I–I–"

"She was looking for something for me," a familiar feminine voice calls from behind. Turning around, I'm surprised to find Sabine standing at the archway of the kitchen. "Looks like you found it too," she says, pointing to the glass ball from earlier at the corner of the cavern hole.

Dane shares a look between us. He's not convinced, but he tightens his mouth, resigning to speak. "Good enough," he grunts, brushing past me. "Better get our lord Grim his meal... "

"Yes, he has worked up quite an appetite," Sabine croons, winking at me while biting the stem of a lotus flower. She keeps a wary gaze on me as I follow Dane, and I cringe thinking of her spending time with the Grim lord, but if she is what he wants, so be it.

A shrill creaking noise whispers like the wind through my chambers as I hear the door open. My nerves swim at the haunting image of Sydney's shadow glowing through the darkness.

Her steps are small, quiet, as she moves deeper into my lair. Although it's not hard to guess the scent of crocus stew permeating the air, it's the sweet smell of this mysterious Specter driving me insane.

Sydney looks around, likely wondering where I am, and I take special note of the smile now etched on her face. Even more curious—I wonder who put it there? It wasn't me. I don't take her as someone who relishes her nights in the kitchen, so what else could curve her delicately pouty lips into such a manner?

The thought burdens my mind, causing me to dig my fingers into the leathery arms of my chair.

"Hello." I choke out the word.

Startled, Sydney tremors, nearly dropping the serving tray, causing the stew to spill a little.

"Frightened?" I churn my tone just enough that it echoes through my chambers.

I watch as Sydney swallows hard. I think of how my hand would feel on her throat as she swallows down everything I have to give, my manhood submerged in that pretty mouth.

"What are you doing in the shadows?" she asks coolly.

Tapping my fingers beneath my chin, I undress her with my eyes. "Thinking of ways to ruin you."

Another gulp. I know I'm getting to her, but she's more stubborn than she appears. I take a deep breath, if only to catch a whiff of her enchanting scent.

"Very well then, my lord." She steps to the side and places the tray down on a small wooden table next to me. "Your meal is ready. Dane said you enjoy a good pot of stew. I do hope so. I made it. This is my family–"

"Where have you been?" I lash out, detecting a strange scent on her.

Her lips crouch to one side. "My lord? I was in the galley making your stew. With Dane?" Sydney's words are more of a question than a statement. Rising from my seat, I take her by the wrist. "And where else have you been? I know the scent of my court."

Pursing her lips tight, Sydney tries but fails to break away from my hold. "Please, my lord. I've already told you."

Pressing her against the wall, my shadows wrap around her as I lean in and take another sniff. I'm pleased not to find any male scent on her, but I still know something is off. There's a dank odor, reminiscent of the old hydra caves, exuding from her. While we've cleared all the old hydras out eons ago, I can think of no reason for her to go there.

"Half truths, and even those are tantamount to lies. Now tell me!" I cup her chin between my fingers, yet still, she holds firm. Taking her shoulders in my hands, I keep my eyes on her. I wish I could see into her eyes, but her tightened mouth lets me know she refuses to say more.

Almost instinctively, shadowy hands yank the straps of her bodice down her arms until her large breasts spill out as a low growl rumbles through me at the delicious sight of her.

Gasping, Sydney leans her head back against the wall. "My lord Grim!" Her back arches, pushing her perky breasts on display.

"That's better," I moan at her neck. "This is how you're supposed to dress in my chambers, remember?"

"Yes, my lord."

Running my hand up her side, I cup one of her breasts in my palm. Circling her nipple with my thumb, I smile as I feel her dampen my finger. "Now, are you going to tell me the truth, or will I have to spank it out of you?"

"What?" she shrieks, turning her head back toward me, her mouth rounded into that perfect O that makes me want to fill it.

"You heard me."

"You wouldn't dare!" she breathes back.

"If you won't give me the truth–" I snatch her by the arm as I fall back into my seat and throw her over my lap. "I'll take on the dare!" I growl, throwing her hood off her back, revealing her perfectly plump backside.

Sydney's ass is perfect, molded perfectly for my hands as I cup the swell of her cheeks popping out from beneath her bodice. Her legs are spread wide, and I can see the outline of her lower lips through the thin lace.

*Shit.* I've dug a hole for myself. The thought makes me half-crazed. Why is she doing this to me?

I crash the palm of my hand against her left cheek, and she cries out, flailing in my grip as her breast bounces against my knee. Her ass pops up in response, perfectly reddened flash appearing beneath the lace, and I think of how I'll kiss it once she learns her lesson.

"That was just the first one. Now, tell me where you've been!" I squeeze her butt hard.

She groans, and I feel wetness on my knee. Her breasts must be leaking. Good. I have her attention.

"In the galley, my lord," she grits out, refusing the truth.

I swipe her opposite cheek this time, and the way it jiggles as I do makes my dick hard. *Fuck.* I didn't think this through. She wiggles against me, and I see her bare sweet spot shining through the fabric.

Keeping my hand on her, I glide my fingers down until I move under the lace to the entrance of her sex. As I do, she moans sweetly, and the sound makes my dick weep with excitement. Wetness crowds her entrance, and I tap my fingers gently between her plump folds.

"My lord, please," she whimpers, and I feel her drip from both her breasts and her sex.

"Please what?" I growl with a hard pat against her slick center. She bounces again, but this time, I think it's deliberate. My finger slides into her sweet little hole, and a willful grunt rips through me. She's softer and wetter than I could ever hope she'd be.

*She is magic.*

Swirling the tip of my finger around, I plunge a little deeper until I find that sensitive nub. I want to stroke it, make it hum for me—just not yet.

"Whatever you want," she cries, desperately wanting me to go further. She wiggles back on my hand, gyrating, trying to climb to a bout of ecstasy, but I won't make it that easy for her.

I stiffen my hand. "I want the truth."

Sydney tries to move again, but I retract my finger and rest my hand on her backside.

"Please! I'll tell you whatever you want to know." I give her backside a little smack. "I saw Hala, that's all," she tearfully confesses.

Damn it. Every time I think there's something brewing between us, I'm reminded this is all for her sister. While my touch may excite her, I'm not buying that this has anything to do with me.

I want to say something, but I can think of nothing. I'm sure as hell not going to put a fucking heart I don't even own on a sleeve for someone who's heart isn't mine.

Groaning, Syd looks over her shoulder, her lips a mixture of pouting and anger. She has no idea how much I want her right now, but I cannot. I will not let her use me to get her fix. I've had enough folk do that over the ages, and I'll not allow that between us.

"What's wrong?" I muster the will to speak. "Is your sweet little hole needy for some attention?"

Her mouth curves into a frown, turning her head away from me. "May I get up, my lord?" she says, pushing up on my knee. Testing my resolve, I take another look at her ass, hopeful to catch a peek of her sex. Thankfully for her, her hood falls against her back, blocking my view.

I help her up, nearly pushing her off me. I'm not sure if she can see how hard I am, but I grab my gown at the edge of my bed, refusing to let her see the power she has over me.

"I'll let you off this time," I snap over my shoulder. "Next time, tell me the first time I ask."

Sydney remains silent. I can tell she's pissed. So be it.

I grab my other gown and wrap it around me. I need to get out of here. If I keep looking at her, there's no telling what I'll do.

My shadows carry me to the door, and I yank at the handle. "I'll be back."

"What about your stew, my lord?"

I look past her at the pot. She seems a bit too eager for me to eat it— it's probably poisoned. "You eat it. I have business to attend to."

"But–"

I let the door slam behind me before I hear anything more.

**G**ame. On. Mr. Grim.

Although I swore I wouldn't let him get the best of me, here I am, literally dripping from every frigging crevice, all because he is a complete control-crazed asshole.

If he thinks I'm going to spend every waking moment in his bedchamber, letting him turn me on and off like a mere flame, then it's time he gets burned.

Not only am I certain he's spinning on the edge, trying to act as though his willpower is stronger than my own, I know better.

I saw him in the shower. I felt him rise beneath me only moments ago, and I can still recall his immediate reaction when I first arrived in his chamber.

He wants me.

Perhaps he thinks a Grim lord is too good for a lowly Specter like me?

Either way, I won't let him toy with me any further. So, I'll give him two options: either outright reject me, which may temporarily bruise my ego, but at least I'll finally know the truth, or bury himself so deep inside me, his shadows will meld with my own.

Whatever the case, before the next watch of the night, I'll know exactly where I stand.

And so will he.

~

I finally finished cleaning out the closet. Moving my supplies to a corner hall, I find a few fabrics in his wardrobe I can use to make a somewhat comfortable resting place. While most Netherfolk don't sleep, Specters like myself often need a margin of rest to fully restore ourselves. Different from our distant Changeling kin, we retain a modicum of lifeblood and need restorative rest like mortals to keep ourselves at our best.

It's probably one of the reasons Scullards like to use my kind to nourish their herds. We're one of the few beings in the Netherworld with lifeblood. Still, I'd rather let the Grim lord send me into his mirth before giving my body to nourish those wretched beings. Their cruelty is beyond repair. The Grim lord may be callous, but the Scullards are without honor. Despite whatever disgust my host has for me, at least he cares enough to restrain himself. The Scullards, on the other hand, know no decency.

The smell of the crocus stew is calling my name, and I decide to answer. The Grim lord may not be hungry enough to eat, but I am. I haven't eaten in quite a while, so I'm famished. I'm surprised that I can taste my own tears in the pot. It gives a sweet and salty flavor that strangely pairs well with the crocus. Not that I plan on crying every time I make this, but it's good to know.

After eating, I decide to pick up the place a little. There's no better way to familiarize myself with a place that will likely become my home than cleaning.

Dusting and wiping down the hard surfaces until I see my own reflection seems to brighten the otherwise macabre dwelling. There's a large silver crest on the wall near the window, covered with cobwebs and soot. The Netherworld is prone to soot storms, and I'm sure it carries into the room from the window. If I had the lungs of mortals, I'm certain I'd be sneezing by now.

The crest is a sugared skull with serpents coiled through the mouth and lips, but it's the nose of the skull pulling my attention. There's etching in ancient Nether tongue encased in an onyx stone that seems familiar to me.

*I've seen this before!*

I gasp, pulling on the cord from my neck.

Horrorstruck, my mind is riddled with confusion as I stare at my father's heirloom and back at the silver crest. Not only is the etching identical, but, holding it against the center of the skull's face, I not only see a faint glowing light, but it looks like the heirloom fits perfectly inside.

Frightened, I pull my hand away before letting the two touch. I have no idea what would happen, and I don't want to be responsible for something catastrophic.

*Crap!*

I wonder if that's why the Grim lord brought me here. Is his goal to get this ring from me?

An even better question is why would my father have a ring like this in the first place?

Perhaps he planned to bargain our lot with the Grim lord using the ring. That is, until he fell for Purcival's scheme. Father always spoke highly of the Grim lord. I recall him saying if he ever needed help, he'd go to him. That's why when I took Hala from Purcival, I came straight here.

Still, it's obvious that the Grim lord wants this ring; I'm surprised he hasn't simply snatched it from around my neck. There's nothing stopping him, or at least, I think so.

Now I know for sure I need to put my plan into action. If the Grim lord only wants me for this ring, he'll discard me the moment he gets it.

I need to give him another reason to keep me here, and that's exactly what I plan to do.

"Get over here!" I hear Roark yell in the distance. The faint sounds of screams from afar let me know I'm close to his lair.

The retching sound of a soul torn asunder leads me around the corner. With his scythe aimed high, the splintered carcass of some now lifeless creature lays at his feet.

"Vagrant filth!" Roark spits on the ground before kicking the withering hull into a large pile near a small footwall.

Standing nearly nine-feet, with a brawn chest of decayed flesh melded with hard bone, the Reaper lord's otherwise grotesque features are enough to frighten any soul, mortal or Nether. Although he presents himself as a hulk-bound giant with long, flowing locks when he's in the high court, this is how most see him–especially when he's busy reaping.

"Well, I see you're at it again," I smile, extending my hand for a greeting.

"Tis the season, I'm afraid," he grumbles, wiping his large jaw before offering his hand in return.

"Yes, yes, I know." I rock on my heel. "The line at the black gate was stretched far beyond what the eye can see."

"Yeah, with Festivus around the corner, there'll be no stopping the leeches seeking your mirth or the vagrants skulking the perimeter of Purgia, but I'll find them," Roark adds, narrowing his gaze around the dark fields near his lair.

"I have no doubt you will, my friend," I say, walking alongside the footwall, admiring the Reaper lord's kill count. "You've been busy." I throw an appreciative smirk his way.

He growls like a hungry bear. "Very." Roark's chest heaves a little, and I can tell he's still in full-on Reaper mode. Not that I'm afraid, but I keep my distance, hopeful he'll cool off soon.

"So," he groans, spitting on the ground once more. "What brings you my way?"

"I was hoping you would hold court with me. That is, if you could stand to take a break."

Roark quirks a brow. "Been a long time since you've asked me to join you." He stares at me like he's awaiting an answer. "Why don't you tell me what this is really about?"

I continue my pacing along the footwall—I don't need my expression to give anything away.

"Well, I've heard some unsettling rumors. I think we should investigate."

Groaning, Roark's chest rumbles. "What kind of rumors?"

"The nefarious kind. The kind that will likely piss off the Great Prince should he hear of it upon his return."

Roark drops the blade of his scythe into the ground—it makes a hard thump as it slices through the dirt near his feet, digging deep into the soil. "Sounds like the kind that needs to be stopped."

I nod. "Indeed."

Roark picks up his scythe and heaves it over his shoulder. "What are we waiting for? Let's bring the rumor mill to court!"

~

On our way to the courtyard, I filled Roark in on what Sydney shared about Purcival's schemes. Much like me, he didn't worry much about Hala becoming a milking wench, but the thought of anyone, especially an esteemed magistrate of the lower court, running a lottery behind our backs is reprehensible.

"So what's the plan? Give him a chance to be honest? Or let 'em choke on his own lies?" Roark asks as we take our seats.

"Let's go with the latter," I sneer over my shoulder, sharing a darkened gaze with my fellow death dealer.

Placing his large palm on my shoulder, Roark gives me another stare, but this time, I can't make it out.

"What?" I shake his hand off me.

He breathes hard, still examining me. "I–I don't know," he pauses, dragging his gaze through the length of me. "Something's different." Narrowing his gaze, he releases a deep groan. "Ah, I see. It's the woman."

Turning away from him, I fold my arms over my chest before letting out a heavy sigh. "Roark, can you please stay focused? They'll be here any moment."

Grabbing my shoulder hard, Roark growls, letting me know he's serious. "I'm not so easily brushed aside, old friend. Now, tell me why this is so important to you."

As he squeezes my shoulder, I wince at the pain, but I keep my eyes fixed on Roark. "Look, I already told you. The woman in my bedchamber told me about the LowLand lottery schemes."

"Yes, and if I know you, old friend, you wouldn't care unless she was of some importance or you thought it threatened your position. So, which is it?"

I let out a sigh, and Roark loosens his grip. "Well, I'm hardly threatened by some LowLand magistrate, if that's what you're wondering."

"And the woman?"

I pause, listening for the door to see if I hear anyone approaching.

Nothing but silence stirs in the courtyard—that and the sound of Roark's heavy breathing at my side, awaiting a response.

"She has a Grim ring," I blurt out. It's not a deliberate lie, but not the truth I know the Reaper lord seeks.

Aghast, he leans away from me. "Impossible!"

I'm thankful for the diversion. "Very possible, I'm afraid."

"Are you sure she isn't a grim? Because if she is—"

I wave a dismissive hand. "Oh please, Reaper! Of course she's not a grim. I think I would know my own kind," I groan at the thought. If Sydney were a grim like me that would stifle every urge I have to claim her for my own. Grim kind cannot lay with Grim kind. It is forbidden. We all come from the same molten mire, making us kindred. To lay with a grim could bring about an oblivion of the worst kind.

I shudder at the thought.

Roark stares at me for a beat before issuing a faux throat clearing to regain my attention. "How did this Specter woman come to have such a thing?"

Pursing my lips tight, I rear back, folding one leg over the other. "That's what I'd like to know. She says it is a family heirloom, but I need to make sure she didn't steal it from Purcival."

Roark groans. "There's no way he'd ever admit to having one. Doing so would all but insinuate his treachery. I mean, orchestrating a lottery of his own is an offense in itself, but claiming a Grim ring for his own is something else entirely."

I nod in agreement. "And now you see my conundrum, dear friend. I can't outright ask him about the ring–especially if he's in cahoots with Hades. Hades knows that by obtaining the ring, I could once and for all end my subjugation to him and restore the full power of mirth to my people. If Purcival is one of his minions, he'd do whatever possible to stop that from happening, including apprising the ruler of the Underworld of my intent."

Rubbing his stubble, Roark's brow twitches. "I see your dilemma. Best to keep her out of sight."

"Precisely."

"But be careful, old friend," Roark begins with a starch and stern tone. "I know just as you that such a ring cannot simply be taken. It must be given, and to do that, you must somehow court this woman to give up something so precious."

"Don't worry, Roark. I know I'll have to win this Specter's heart if I ever hope to obtain the ring."

"We are death dealers, Thelios. Matters of the heart are not our specialty. We barter and reap. That is our lot. To take a soul is fair game. To win a heart, however, is the biggest gamble of all."

Once more, silence sits between us as the weight of his words haunt me.

I've complicated things with Sydney more than I'd hoped. How do I tell the one who vacates souls how the weightless hole in my chest feels full when Sydney is near? Or that even now, I long to be where she is, if for no other reason than to pant in the shadow of her steps.

The loud sound of the door swinging open as the grates hit against the stone wall release me from my musing.

"Grim and Reaper will see you now," Dane announces as Roark and I sit up in our seats.

"My lords," Purcival calls, dropping to one knee with a hand on his chest.

"Step forward," Roark begins, waving Purcival and his right hand, Amarok, forward.

Seeing Purcival, a once esteemed griffin, walk with the likes of Amarok, a flesh-eating Scullard, is enough to make my lips curve in disgust. Even more, the thought of him doing anything to harm Sydney, or even her sister Hala, muddles my mind with murderous intent.

"There have been rumors running amuck," I start, shooting Amarok a dark glare as I watch his eyes search the courtyard. No doubt he's looking for Sydney. "And we need you to sort them out."

Purcival nods, his two gray wings flapping at his back as his lion-like features work hard to feign endearment. "However I may be of service, my lords."

Roark gives me a look, slightly rolling his eyes. Neither of us are buying the bull Purcival is selling. "You can start by telling us what you know of lottery scalpers and black ships not commissioned by the Ferryman himself."

Purcival swallows deep, his gold mane shifting in the wind blowing through the courtyard. Amarok snarls, looking up at Purcival as if he's warning him to remain quiet. Roark and I share another look—it's obvious Purcival may not be the one in charge.

"Sir Purcival," I call out, hoping to lure his attention away from the daring gaze of Amarok.

"Y–Yes, my lord." He swallows hard, tightening the clasp of his fist at his waist. "I'm afraid to say I know nothing of any black ships."

"And what of lottery scalping?" Roark barks as soon as Purcival gets the words out of his mouth.

He takes a deep breath. Rocking on his hind legs, Purcival looks over his shoulder to Amarok. "What of it, my lord?" he says with a nonchalant shrug. "I only tend to those not eligible for your lottery and assigned to the LowLand. If there is another lottery, I know nothing of it."

Groaning, I feel my patience waning. "Will you swear it on your own soul?"

"I–I–"

"Be careful how you answer, griffin!" Roark growls, running his hands over his scythe laying on the table in front of him. "Your next words could be your last."

"Yes, and anyone found participating in treason against the Great Prince will not find the grace of either mine or Reaper's scythe."

Roark laughs darkly. "No." His shoulders roll in amusement. "That would be too great a grace."

I let out a wicked chortle of my own. "Too great indeed!" I continue laughing, rubbing my boney fingers together.

Tremors ripple through Purcival as he exchanges nervous glances between us and Amarok.

Leaning back in his seat, Roark's half-skeleton, half-rotten flesh face gleams as darkness dances in his soulless eyes. "Spit it out, LowLand! Tell us how you swear fealty to the Great Prince and would never do anything to warrant being cast into the Fountain."

Running to our table, Purcival drops to his knees, trembling before us. "Please, my lords!" he cries out. "It was him–" he exclaims, pointing to Amarok over his shoulder. "That mangy Scullard Beast is in league with Hades and perhaps even the Changelings!"

"You wretch!" Amarok balks, charging toward Purcival. Before he has a chance to reach him, though, Roark commands two of his dark guards to restrain him. "You will regret your cowardice!"

"Well, well," I chuckle, turning to Roark. "Plot twist."

Nodding in agreement, Roark smiles. "A most surprising one."

With a shriek, my face contorts into a ghastly dark hole. "Tell us the truth!" I shout, banging my scythe at my side.

"It's Amarok and the Scullards, my lords. They compelled me to send the lowly ones to the black ships, but these ships do not carry to Hades alone," Purcival confesses, and Roark raises a brow in surprise. "The Scullards feast on the lowly ones before sending them to the Underworld. It's a heinous act, I know, but they compelled me!" he cries, lifting his hands in surrender as he bows before us.

Lowering his scythe to Purcival's chin, Roark lifts him up by the tip of his blade. "And how do they compel you, LowLand?" Roark challenges him, not convinced.

Looking over his shoulder, Purcival gives Amarok one last look. Seething, Amarok grinds his sharp teeth together, spit dripping to his furry chin as he struggles in the hold of the dark guard.

"I–I was promised a place in Hades' court if I could procure a Grim ring—but I would never, never steal from you, great one!" Purcival cries.

"Of course you wouldn't," I snarl, leaning into him. The smell of his cowardice sickens me.

Roark lifts his chin once more, digging deeper into Purcival's jugular. "Tell us."

"There was a man–he had two daughters. I promised them safe passage via the lottery, and—" His voice lowers as Roark thrusts the scythe in a little more. We know it won't kill him, but it *will* make him talk. "He had a ring. I was told to give it to—"

"You traitor!" Amarok shouts, breaking free of the dark guard's hold. "You will pay! You will all pay!" Thrashing a wad of onyx sand to the ground, Amarok gnashes his teeth at us and spins his heel in the sand, disappearing from our view.

"Search the grounds for him!" Roark orders to the guard, who scurries quickly from our view.

Yanking Purcival up by his collar, I snarl as I pull him to his feet. "Who were you supposed to give the ring to?"

"Hades, my lord!" he confesses immediately. "His power is waning. He needs it to withstand the tyranny of the Changelings. It was never about deceiving you, sire, I swear it!" Purcival crumples his chin to his shoulder, sulking in fear.

"And the woman?" I growl in his ear, thankful Roark is still too busy ordering the guards around.

"C–Collateral, sire. Mere collateral. But the girl—Hades said I could have her as long as she kept the Scullards nourished."

Fuck. Everything Syd told me was true.

Releasing Purcival from my hold, I bang my scythe against the ground. *"Mors obitus y tu mal,"* I whisper as I watch my shadows gather from my sides, gripping Purcival by his arms. "Into darkness you shall be," I sneer, banging the rod deeper into the hollow below.

I watch as a murky funnel forms around Purcival, pulling him bit by bit into my mirth. He cries out, pleading for mercy, but little does he know, whatever mercy I have left belongs to one person, and he'll never hurt her again.

Since the Grim lord is taking longer than expected to return, I decide to take a quick rinse in his shower. While I'm not certain whether he'll mind, what's the worst he could do to me?

The waterfall shower is magic! I'm sure it flows from the remaining body of water separating us from the earthbound realm. Each drop of water upon my skin feels like a sensual caress—maybe that's why the Grim lord was so overtaken when I spied him wrangling the venomous monster between his thighs.

Noticing the remnants of what he left behind on the walls and floor makes me envious of the stone walls and floor of his shower. Although I can't be sure, I bet he'd enjoy the softer places I'd gladly give him.

And therein lies my problem.

Being at his disposal.

I need to ensure I can't be so easily tossed aside. I need to give him a reason to *want* to keep me near. Not only do I fear what losing my place in his bedchamber could mean for me, I worry even more what it could mean for Hala. I can't let her fall into the hands of Purcival ever again.

I'm out of the shower quickly, and I fold as much of the hooded cape over myself as I can. Making a note that we'll need more towels in the future, I grab the Grim lord's towel from the edge of his bed.

It smells like him, like leather and smoke.

The scent is inviting, reminding me of how he looked at me as I dried him off after his shower. From the feel of his chiseled chest beneath the terry cloth to the view of the thick, veiny monster between his thighs aimed at me, to even the seductive dance of his serpents as their forked tongues leapt toward me, my body warms at the thought of him.

My breasts leak, and my mind replays how good it felt to have his thumb circling my nipples, how he groaned when he sucked his finger. Looking around the room, there's not a place my eyes can travel without thinking of him.

Rushing into the closet, I figure this is the one place the haunting memories of him won't follow me. This is the place–the disheveled hole in the wall–that he tauntingly told me would be my resting place. Even his tone was cruel and callus–without a care, even, when he goaded me inside after making me believe he wanted to have sex with me.

Still, even standing inside this once dank dungeon, I can't shake the thought of him. Dropping to the floor, I curl onto the pallet of soft fabrics I found in his lair. Holding his towel over me, I massage my breast, hopeful to relieve the ache gnawing within me.

But that's not the only part aching.

So, I reach between my legs.

I've been the only one caring for my own bouts of passion these days. Sometimes, I can make the climb, and other times, it isn't so easy. Normally, Hala is sleeping near me, so that is a distraction all by itself, but for once, I'm alone, left with nothing but thoughts of a Grim lord who is repulsed by a Specter like me.

Sure, he's obviously aroused by the sight of my breasts and my form, but, like most men, he likely assumes only a monster resides under my hood. In that, he is correct. I am a monster, a wraith of the darkest kind. My gaze alone sends anyone into such a hell-like suspension, I'm forced to keep my eyes covered. It's no wonder the Grim lord is doing all he can to stay clear of me. That's probably why he's been gone for so long.

*Then again...*

I remember his touch, the swipe of his hand against my rear. The touch of his thick finger between my folds. The knock of his hardened member on my abdomen as I laid across his lap.

Moaning, I swirl my finger around the slippery slope of my entrance, working that sensitive nub into a fit until I've had my release. Mewling, panting noises are all I can muster as I drive desirous thoughts of the Grim lord's nakedness forward in my memory.

"Keep going," I hear a dark and lush voice whisper.

Startled, I sit up on my elbows, surprised to find the Grim lord now staring down at me. He seems bigger than usual as he towers over me at the closet door, but that's not what disturbs me most.

It's the sight of his boney palm stroking his length beneath his gown that has me in a frenzy.

"My–my lord," I call out, desperately looking for the towel I hadn't noticed fell off. When I notice it on my side, the Grim lord stomps his foot hard, pulling the towel away with his heel.

"Oh no you don't," he warns, wagging a skeleton finger in my direction. "What did I tell you?"

I shrug, using what I can of my cape to cover up. "I–I'm sorry, my lord. I–"

"What did I tell you?" he lashes out, his voice echoing through his chamber as he leans over me. I watch as his face slowly transforms, flesh covering bone as he stares into my eyes.

"Sire, I don't understand," I reply, unsure what he is referring to.

Bending so that he's now sniffing near the nape of my neck, he snarls, the snakes wandering beneath his sleeves hissing at me. Taking a deep breath, he exhales, and a sweet, smoky scent invades my nostrils, making me feel like I just took a hit of lotus flower.

"What did I say I would do if I saw that pretty little nighthole between your legs?" he breathes against my neck. "Tell me!" he barks, making my body shudder in response.

I'm shaking, breasts leaking, wetness pooling at my center as I quake under the thunderous call of his voice. "You–you said you would fuck me into oblivion, sire." My voice is quiet, but I know he heard me.

Standing upright, the Grim lord removes his gowns. This time, he's not as meticulous as before. Nearly throwing his garments over his shoulder, he looms over me, his large manhood aimed in my direction as he strokes his need.

"Open," he commands, knocking my legs apart with a swipe of his knee.

I do as he instructs, fearful the sight of how much I'm leaking will disgust him.

"Mmm..." he groans, licking his lips as his eyes travel over the entirety of my body. "Lay back so I can see everything." His heavy tone sweeps over me in one breath, and I'm on my back before I can even think of anything else.

Once more, he uses his knee to pry my legs apart. This time, though, fire blazes in his eyes as he watches me. As he drops between my legs while still holding his large shaft, the ravenous look in his eyes makes me tremble.

Instinctively, I draw my knees together, fearful of the dangerous look in his eyes, but he grabs my legs and pushes them wide.

Here I am, laid bare before the Grim lord of the Netherworld. My heart is nearly jumping out of my chest while my sex is doing somersaults, hopeful of what comes next.

Licking his lips, he moans once more as his eyes stay locked at my core. "I've never seen such a pretty little pussy in all my nights. Bare. Ripe. Plump in all the right places. You're so fucking wet, I can practically see my own reflection."

"Ah..." I whimper. "What do you see, my lord?"

"I see the darkness in you... and it is beautiful." Pausing, the Grim lord brushes a gentle finger over my folds, and I nearly combust at his touch. "Look at you, leaking everywhere," he grunts, one hand gripping my knee hard. "Tell me, sweetness, what's got you so worked up?" Before I can part my lips to speak, he lifts a finger in warning. "And remember what I told you earlier about giving me the truth the first time I ask it. Now, tell me."

"You," I tearfully confess, wishing I was stronger than how feeble I must look right now. "I was thinking of you."

A devious curl hovers at the corner of his lips as he leans over me. "And what were you thinking?"

"You were gone so long, my lord," I say. I want to tell him I thought of him naked, but I can't.

He grabs my sex hard, and with a pouty lip and darkened eyes, he moans. "Aww, so she's weeping?"

"Huh?" I question, but I don't have a chance to say more before he plunges a finger inside me. "My lord!" I cry out when he forces a second finger inside.

"Ah... that's it, sweetness. Let me wipe all that longing away." His fingers thrust in and out of me, his heavy shaft pressed against my abdomen as he kisses my neck. With his free hand, he grabs one of my breasts. "I've been dying to have these in my mouth," he grunts, biting my nipple before sucking my breast into his mouth. Flicking his tongue against the sensitive skin, he sucks hard, like he's trying to drain me dry.

With my head reared back and my spine arched, the feel of him pressed against me has me desperate for him in ways I never knew I could feel. I don't know if seeing me naked just made him throw caution to the wind, but whatever the reason, I'm thankful.

Fear trickles up my spine, warning me that this may be a one-time thing. Perhaps he'll throw me aside entirely after this, but I refuse to live in a place of doubt. I need this too much.

I do this not for Hala, but for me.

If but only for a moment, I need to feel wanted and adored. I want to be held and ravaged. He can drain every drop from me, as long as my body is relieved of the ache it so desperately needs to rid itself of.

The Grim lord's fingers war over my sex, and I feel my climax bubble within me. My core tightens, and my body goes limp under his masterful touch.

"Come for me," he orders, and my body willfully obeys his command, enjoying the cool feel of his breath between my breasts.

Cackling, he laughs in such a melodious yet malevolent manner as he holds a hand on my stomach, the other on my sex. I convulse in his grip, leaking from all parts, like an endless spring around him.

"That's it, love," he coos, gently running his hand down my neck, between my breasts, down my stomach. "You needed this," he says, almost sweetly, and I have to open my eyes to make sure it's him as I come down from my high. "And so did I," he groans, pulling his fingers from my sex and plunging them into his mouth.

Closing his eyes, he rests his fingers between his lips, savoring my taste.

"Thank you, my lord," I say, just thankful to finally have my needs met. "How can I repay you?"

His eyes pop open, and this time, I see the same fire from before brewing behind his eyes. "Let me show you."

I have never seen such a beautiful creature in my entire existence. The way her body responds to me, like it was made for me, is mesmerizing.

When I came back from dealing with Purcival's treachery, I had every intention to tell her she no longer needed to be subject to my bedchamber. She and Hala could remain in Purgia as citizens without owing any debts. But when I found her touching herself to orgasm in the closet of my own bedchamber, I had to seize the opportunity.

Sure, I considered how granting her freedom could entreat her to give me the Grim ring, but I wanted her safe more. Now that I've seen how well her body yields to my touch, I just have to see how far this goes.

Rising back to my knees, I pry her legs open once more. Why she insists on shielding herself from me, I don't know, but every time she does, I'll remind her how I need to see her.

My dick in hand, I rub the crown against her entrance, letting her wetness glide over me, and I nearly combust at the feel of her greedy little pussy trying to pull me in.

Then, it hits me. "You *want* me to fuck you?"

She nods eagerly. "Yes, my lord. Please," she whines, lifting her hips so I'm once more aligned with her entrance.

Shit. I don't know how long I can contain myself.

"Why?" I bark, and she quivers, her large breasts bouncing as she tries to push back, but I grab her ankle, bringing her back to me.

My crown nudges inside her soft sex as her plump lower lips cover the tip.

"I've wanted you since I came into your chamber, my lord."

"That's not an answer!" I growl, my dick throbbing, begging me to power forward.

I feel her wetness gather around me, and I watch as shimmering embers drip from her breasts. Syd's pretty mouth scrunches to one side as she bites her lip, trying her best to keep her secrets.

"It's you, my lord!" she finally fires back. "The way you talk, the way you look at me–like you want me. No one ever looks at me, no one sees me. But you—you've never seen my eyes, and I feel like you see me. You saw me when I came to your court. You saw me when I bared myself to you in your bedchamber. And even now–you see me. You have no idea what it's like, my lord, to be seen!"

*What the hell...*

Dropping my hands from my shaft, I take her head in my hands. Looking at her, albeit just her mouth and the small bridge of her nose, I feel something I've never felt before.

"What are you doing to me?" I say, adding a small kiss to her chin, and she folds into me, wrapping her long legs around my waist. Once more, her hips raise, and I feel her pulling me inside her. "Syd," I begin, one hand now circling her breast. "You know there's no way I can fuck you now, right?"

Her mouth parts into that pretty little *O*, and I plunge my thumb inside before she can protest. Shaking my head, I lean my forehead against hers as I realign myself at her entrance. Gasping, she drops her head to my shoulder as she feels me gently settle inside her.

"At least, not here." I grunt, lifting her in my arms and carrying her to my bed. Syd's eyes grow wide in amazement as I lay her perfect body down. "That's right, sweetness. I need to do something I never thought I would do: make love to you, right here, right now. You belong in my bed. Do you understand?"

"Yes, my lord!" she cries out as small droplets race to her chin.

Syd barely has the words out of her mouth before I'm sinking into the softest, wettest pussy I've ever known. The way she wraps her legs around me forces me to drive forward so deep, I feel like I'm losing myself in a dark abyss.

Dark, shadowy arms rise from my sides, holding Sydney's arms and legs so she is fully spread out, but she doesn't flinch. Instead, she relaxes within their touch like she was waiting for them.

"You like that?" I whisper as I slam into her sleek center. "You like the feel of my shadows touching you?"

Nodding her head in agreement, she whines as a shadowy palm claws at her breast.

"Wrap me in your shadow," she moans as I grind deep. "Fill me with your darkness."

I can feel her walls tighten around me, but I find new depths and walls to break. I hold onto my emerald stone headboard, pounding hard and fast until I tear every fucking wall down, both hers and mine.

Her doubts. Her fears. I'll grind away every fucking hurtful place until they're replaced with the hope of what we can be to and for one another.

Sydney meets my thrusts as if she has her own ax to grind, swirling her hips in rhythm with mine as her bountiful breasts bounce against my chest. I pull one into my mouth, sucking and fucking in one fluid motion.

But I need more.

Pulling out of her, I flip Syd to her knees. She quickly pulls the cape of her hood to the side, giving me a full view of her perfect ass and her sweet little slit. I still see the red mark from her earlier spanking, and I press my mouth to it. Parting her cheeks wide, I run my thumb over that dark little hole. She flinches, but I hold her waist still.

"Every hole of yours is now mine," I growl at her back, and I feel her relax some. "That's my good girl." I give her one long lick, from her dark little hole down through her sweet spot, until my mouth is feasting on her sex. From this angle, I can alternate between holes, never giving her a moment's relief.

"My lord Grim!" she cries out as I feel her spasm against my tongue.

Repositioning myself behind her, I plunge my dick into her slick center without warning, and she cries out once more. "Thelios!" I grunt, driving my hard length into her.

She looks over her shoulder, her pouty lips parting. *I'll fill that mouth soon enough*.

"Thelios!" I repeat my name. "You will call me Thelios!"

Quaking in my grip as I offer blow after blow, she cries out. "Thelios!"

"That's right, sweetness!" I roar, slamming into her. "If you can take my dick, you can take my name!" With one final thrust, I'm coming, so hard that I see nothing but blackness, and Syd squeals with a small chuckle.

Slowly, I open my eyes, still in a daze. My two familiars are stretching out from me, now wrapped around Sydney. "What the fuck?" I quirk a brow, surprised to see both serpents now latched on to her breasts. I've never seen them do that before. "En Cala! En Serif!" I shout their respective names as they hiss at me before tethering back to my skin, I give both snakes a look of warning. "Are you okay, sweetness?"

As I gently pull out, she turns over, falling to her back, and I growl at my familiars when I notice the puncture marks on her breasts. "I'm okay," she giggles. "I guess they like me too."

"Greedy little fucks wanted a taste of what's mine!" I grouse, banging a heavy hand over my chest, warning them to stay put.

"Well, they're a part of you, right?" she asks, and I give her a nod. "So I suppose they have a right to me too."

My chest rumbles as I watch the snakes tether back into my skin. "We'll see about that," I say, rolling to my side to admire her. "But really, are you okay?"

"Better than okay, my lord." She nods with a small smile as she circles her finger over my chest.

"Thelios," I repeat my name, and she covers her mouth and lowers her head. Smiling, I lift her chin with my fingers. "We just made love, beauti-ful. You can call me Thelios."

"*Thelios,*" she says so sweetly, I want to kiss her. "That's your name?"

"Yes. Do you like it?"

"It suits you," she answers, still outlining my tattoos with her hand.

I let out a breath. "You're very good at evading questions. I asked if you liked it."

Syd twists her mouth to one side. "Well, what would you do if I didn't? Change it?"

*Smart ass.* Explains why I'm falling for her.

"Only for you," I laugh. Taking Sydney in my arms, I pull her close. The feel of her naked body pressed against my own is something I've wanted from the moment I laid eyes on her, I could hold her like this forever. "Are you sure you're okay?" I ask, lifting her chin once more. I wish I could see her eyes.

"Yes, my–I mean, Thelios. I'm more than okay."

"I'm sorry they bit you," I say, palming her breasts. "I hope it didn't hurt too badly."

Shaking her head, she smiles, biting her fingernail. "It didn't hurt, really. It felt... well, nice."

This is a surprise. "Well, that's never happened before."

"Never?"

I dip my head to hers. "Never." Her mouth parts like she wants to say something, but she presses her lips tight. "I suppose they really took a liking to you, and I can understand why, but what just happened—you know—between us—" I'm fumbling my words now like an idiot.

"Thelios, it's okay. I mean, I understand if this is just a one-time thing."

I give her shoulders a squeeze. "This is not a one-time thing."

With her arms tight in my grasp, Syd's mouth falls open once more. Her head bobs side to side, likely hoping I'll loosen the reins. "As I was saying. I know I'm here to serve your needs in the bedchamber, so if this is to be the way, perhaps we should—"

Just when I was beginning to lessen my grip, I tighten my hold. "Abso-lutely. The Fuck. Not!" I shout. With only a deep, rumbling growl, I scoop Sydney up and toss her over my shoulder.

"Thelios!" she screams, pounding her small fists at my back. "Put me down!"

I've enjoyed lying next to her, but what I have to say next requires us to be eye-to-eye.

Pushing back against my headboard, I straddle Sydney around my waist. The way her breasts bounce as she settles in my lap makes me glad she's all mine. When my already-hard member flicks against her sweet spot, the little grunt she gives almost makes me forget what angered me in the first place.

"Lorna Sydney," I say, working in a very convincing stern tone. I watch as Syd gazes around the room, likely drawn by the rousing echo of my voice. "You are mine, but not just my bedchamber–"

"Am I to join Sabine in the harem now?"

A hearty chuckle rolls through me. "Of course not. I don't need a harem. I have you."

"As your bed wench?" Her chin drops to her chest.

"Lorna Sydney," I say her name stronger this time, and she lifts her face. "If you let that pretty little chin drop once more, I'll impale you on my dick so hard, you'll see stars." She gasps at my words. "Then I'll fuck that pretty little mouth of yours," I add, trailing my thumb along her bottom lip.

"Well, that doesn't sound so bad." She shrugs her shoulders, goading me. *Damn.*

Lifting her at the waist, I align her with my erection, inching her down until we are one flesh.

*Thelios gave me the stars*. And perhaps the moon, too.

My face is aimed high, back arched, breasts bouncing as I ride the Grim lord like a jockey. He has no idea I always wanted to make love in that position, and now, I have.

Although I can tell I'm not the only one enjoying our lovemaking—between palming my rear like a mad man and sucking hard at my breasts, Thelios seems just as entranced by me as I am by him. While I can't be entirely sure, something tells me he wants more from me than being his resident bed wench.

My head rests on his broad shoulders as he nestles me in his arms, laying in complete peace as one his familiars gives gentle licks to the side of my face. The way he holds me, like he never wants to let me go, makes me feel secure and safe. I never thought I'd feel such love in the arms of the Grim lord, but here I am.

Everything in me wants to remove my hood, to show him my true self so that we can be one, but I'll not risk whatever this is by jumping the gun.

"Listen, Syd," Thelios begins, slowly pulling me from his hold. "We need to talk." His voice has changed—it's somber, like something is wrong.

"It's okay, Thelios. Just tell me."

"Argh!" he growls. "Alright, here goes. Purcival is no longer a problem."

I gulp—*hard*. "What?" I lean back. "What do you mean no longer a problem?"

"Reaper and I held court. Purcival admitted to his deeds against your family and about the lottery. Now, he is gathered to my mirth."

Before I have a chance to think, I jump up from his lap. A million thoughts race to my mind, but words fail to form in my mouth. "That's where you've been this whole time?"

Thelios stands up. "Yes," he says with his head lowered.

I hadn't noticed how young he looks. With the way his hair is cut alongside his jawbone, there's an innocence to him I've never seen before. It's no wonder I've been so worked up. He is gorgeous!

"Look, Syd, I wanted to tell you, but when I got here—"

"We made love," I whisper, finishing his sentiment. His eyes dart to me, and I swear, I spy a small flame.

"Yes," he groans in response. "Do you hate me? Do you feel I took advantage?"

"My lord, no!" I protest, closing the small distance between us, placing a finger over his lips. "That is..." I begin, fumbling with the heirloom around my neck. "Was it only your intent to have this?" I

"Of course not!" He bats my hand away. "Purcival admitted to wanting to steal it from you. I'll not trade you one schemer for the next."

My eyes water. I can hardly believe my ears. He's not the horrid soul I thought he was.

Closing his palm over my hand, he pushes my clenched fist back to my chest. "This belongs with you."

"But my lord–"

"Thelios," he corrects quickly, his mouth forming a hard line.

"My lord Thelios," I add. "Look, I know this ring has something to do with—" I go to point at the wall.

Thelios squeezes his palm around my fist. "None of this is about the ring, Sydney. *It's about you.* Now that Purcival is gone, you are free. You and Hala. I'll not hold you captive in my bedchamber. You may both reside in Purgia as you please."

Squealing, I throw my arm around Thelios' neck, kissing him hard. "Thank you, my lord!"

Pulling away, he lowers his head, his countenance fallen.

"My lord?" I say, lifting his chin. "What is it?"

"I'm glad you are happy." He feigns a smile before backing away. Once more sinking down into his chair, he plucks at his fingers with his arms folded across his chest.

"And you, my lord?" I begin, pushing his leg and arms aside so I can sit on his lap. His body is stiffer now than before, and I'm not sure he wants me this close, but I don't care. I turn his head toward me. "What's wrong?"

"You're changing me, that's what," he grouses, narrowing his eyes, trying hard to return to his broody ways. It's not working.

Still, I'll play along. "How so?"

"For starters, you made me renege on my promise."

"What promise?" Now I'm confused.

"To fuck you into oblivion."

A tingling sensation runs up my spine, and I feel my nipples harden. "Well, isn't that what we—"

"No, sweetness, we made love. I promise, if I fucked you, you'd know."

Thelios gives me a hard stare, and I can all but breathe as I feel his hard length jut against my rear. Swallowing hard, I close my eyes, taking in another dose of his enchanting scent and trying to focus on the point of the conversation.

"Was there something else, my lord?"

Now, he's running his hands along my side, and I fear he'll grab my breast, and we'll be *not-fucking* once more. Not that I'd mind, but I want to know what has changed his mood.

"Seeing as Purcival is no longer a problem, you're free to go. You have no need to stay in my bedchamber any longer. You can go and be with your sister."

I grab his chin and lift his face to mine. "Is that it, Thelios? You *want* me to stay?"

"I told you, I'll not force you to do anything. I won't be what Purcival was to you–"

Taking his face between my hands, I pull him in for a kiss. His tongue collides with mine, sweeping gently around my mouth, leaving no part untouched.

Once again, the same magnetism from before locks us in place as he keeps his lips pressed against my own. Faint hissing sounds swim around us as his serpents slither up his arms until they reach my wrists, binding us together.

A small chuckle escapes me. "Well, maybe these guys are intent on keeping me here," I whisper against his mouth.

Thelios shakes his head. "That's not how that works, sweetness," he begins, pulling back some. "They only act on how I'm feeling."

"What about before? When they sucked my—"

"Makes sense. I'm always thinking of gorging myself on these," he growls, pulling my left breast into his mouth.

"I'm not going anywhere!" I cry out, enjoying the lap of his tongue against my nipple.

Burying his head between my breasts, Thelios groans. Looking up at me, he smiles a sexy, devious grin that has my sex pooling once more. "Oh, the things you'll say in a moment of passion."

Pushing back a little, just enough so I can think straight, I run my hand through his hair. As I do, his familiars coil around my arms and neck, licking me along the way.

"Listen, I have no desire to leave you. I want to be here with you, but not as your wench. As your woman."

"You already are," Thelios says matter of factly. "I just needed to know you wanted to be mine."

"Of course we'll need to work out something with Hala," I begin.

"One step ahead of you. I already asked Roark to inform Pella. She'll keep Hala with her until you're ready. I can have Dane make a place for her on the west side of my courtyard. That way, you will be together, but you'll be here with me."

"So you've already worked this out, eh?" I laugh, and he nods with a proud smirk. "Then why were you so sad?"

"I didn't know if you'd want to stay. I mean, how was I to be sure you weren't merely screwing me for your sister's sake?"

"Because I didn't come for Hala, my lord Grim. I came for you. Only you."

# CHAPTER 17

# Thelios

"**D**amn, woman. You are perfect!" Crushing my mouth to Syd's once more stirs feelings of hope inside me that I've never known.

Syd pulls back, tilting her head away from me as she bites her lip. "This is all going so fast," she whispers, still looking away. "It seems like only a moment ago that I was in your court, begging for a pardon–and now, here we are."

Firming my arm around her waist, I pull her close, forcing her to return her attention to me. "Well, let's see. If we were in the earthbound plane, we'd span about at least two years from the moment you came into my court until now."

Biting her fingernail, she gives me a shy smile. "I suppose you're right."

We both laugh at the thought. Time works differently in the Netherworld. Without the sun's influence, our lives drag by. Before Kharon left for the earthbound plane, we were just planning Festivus. Now, we're just about one night watch away from the big day.

"So you see, sweetness, we've already been an item for two years, or at the very least living together," I continue with a laugh, adding a small kiss to her chin.

"But how can you want me to be yours when you've never seen my face?" she mumbles, pulling at her hood.

I still her hand, tugging her wrist until her palm is resting in mine. "We'll cross that bridge when the time is right. There's no rush. Besides, I already know there's nothing under your hood that will change how I feel."

"But–"

I place my hand over her lips. "Shh... Enough about that. You're mine. End of story."

"End of story," she repeats, giggling as she shakes her head.

"Now, I wasn't sure we'd get this far, but I have a surprise for you."

"A surprise?"

"Yes, but you'll have to get dressed. As much as I adore seeing you naked, I think it's best we keep you covered once we step out of my chambers."

A wide grin stretches across Sydney's face. "Where are we going?" she asks, rubbing her hands together.

"I already told you: it's a surprise. Now, go put on your things, and I'll do the same."

～

S ydney is dressed and eagerly standing at my side in no time.

"I need you to do something for me."

"Anything," she says, looking up at me with a warm smile.

Kissing the top of her head, I breathe her in, thankful just to have her close. "Even though your head is covered, I need you to put a hand over your eyes. No peeking."

84

Waving a hand around, Syd smiles again. "Oh, okay." She nods cautiously.

Walking toward the back terrace, I push my knuckle into the wall where my Grim skull sits. I notice that it's cleaner than I remember. Looking around, I notice the entire suite is immaculate. No doubt Syd kept herself busy cleaning while I was out. I'll have to thank her later.

Pressing my hand into the Grim skull, I read the etching across the frame. *Mea Tenebris Eternus Amor.* I don't think I ever noticed it before. Does that mean what I think it does? No, it can't mean–

"Come on!" Syd squeals at my side, pulling my arm. "I can't take the suspense!"

Brushing off the need to think too hard about the meaning of the inscription, I lead us through the terrace doors. A husky wind sweeps around us, closing the doors just as we step over the threshold into a dark cloud. The gale force carries us deep into the murky flume as it opens to a new gateway.

"What was that?" Sydney shrieks, locking her arm around mine.

I let out a small chuckle. "Ah, yes. It gets a tad windy out here. Come now, open your eyes."

Sydney pulls her hand from her eyes as her mouth parts wide in wonder. "Where are we?" she coos, looking around.

"It's my C.O.R., my Chamber of Reflection. The ancients called it a Trux Thalamum, or Grim Chamber. It's a place I go to memorialize those in my mirth. It's where I feel safe," I quietly confess.

Sydney's jaw hangs low as her sweet lips form the perfect oval that makes me think there's something fluttering in my chest. "It's beautiful!" she gasps as she squeezes her small hand in mine, looking around.

I stand in silence, watching as her gaze travels from the large onyx stones to the stream of molten lava flowing through the chamber.

"What are these?" she asks, pointing to a large wall covered in gold ivy.

I smile. "Ah, yes, my favorite part. This is where the names of those in my mirth are captured."

Looking up at me and back at the wall, she frowns. "But I don't see anything."

Yanking a layer from my cloak, I press it against the wall. "Here, hold it like this," I begin.

Syd chuckles as she places her hands under mine. "It feels like papyrus, but how? You just ripped it from your–"

I raise a brow and smile. "Nether-magic, my dear," I answer with a wink.

"Of course," she says.

"I suppose if I were mortal, I'd need a chalky substance, but my fingers will suffice. Now, press my forefinger firmly along the wall and rub. Hard."

Sydney does as I instruct as I guide her hand in a horizontal pattern, back and forth.

"Nethers me!" Syd squeals, quickly gesturing her head toward the wall as the names of the troll and Purcival appear like fiery dust.

"I suppose it's a type of grave rubbing of sorts."

Ogling the wall, Syd glances her hands over the mountainous feature, trailing her petite fingertips along the names. "This is magnificent! All of this!" she exclaims, turning around. "It's so–so–beautiful! I never thought–"

I grab her wrist and pull her back to me. "What? Never considered there was beauty in death?"

She shakes her head. "No, my lord."

"Yes. Life—in whatever form, be it Nether or earthbound—is in fact precious. But those who depart do not lose their value. Memorializing their life ensures their life has meaning."

Syd frowns, turning her head away from me. "Even Purcival?"

I take her chin between my fingers, admiring how adorable her pouted lips look. "Yes, sweetness, even Purcival, for it was his duplicity that brought you to me. If his wretched life served no other purpose than bringing us together, I'll forever be grateful."

A lone, dark tear drops to Syd's chin. "Damn. I never thought something like this was possible."

"What? Being grateful for Purcival?"

She chuckles. "No–well, yes–but us."

I pull her into my embrace. "That makes two of us."

Before I have a chance to relish the feel of her body so close to mine, she once more pulls away. "But what about my father? His name is not here! And the others who Purcival and Amarok tricked."

"Amarok?" I step back. "What do you know of him?"

Syd shrugs her shoulders almost nonchalantly. "Well, he's the Scullard who aligned himself with Purcival to trick my father and the others aboard that ship. In fact, I believe he handpicked Hala for the sole purpose of having her nourish his wretched Scullard horde!" she sneers, her lips curling in disgust.

Folding my arms, I walk along the side of the stream, running my hand through the molten river.

"Thelios?" Syd takes small steps beside me. "What's wrong?"

I force out a sigh. A gnawing feeling in my gut knows something is wrong. Standing, I wipe my hands together, brushing the ash from my palms.

"It's Amarok."

"What about him?"

Taking a deep breath, I take Sydney's hand in mine. "Earlier today, when Reaper and I held court, Amarok was there with Purcival. While Purcival admitted to his treachery, it was Amarok who balked at his cowardice."

Sydney's hand goes cold, and her skin pales to an almost translucent tone. "Amarok was there?" Her voice is too quiet, no more than a whisper.

"Yes." I want to say more to make her feel at ease, but I know there's nothing I can say.

Her head ticks toward me while her lips curve into a faint smile. "So you gathered Purcival into your mirth, and Reaper... did he vacate Amarok's soul?"

I close my eyes, thankful I cannot see in full the disappointment on her face, but I know better, and so does she. "No," I answer. "He had onyx sand and disappeared before we could–"

"No!" Shrieking, Syd steps away from me, breaking from my hand. The sound she makes pierces my ears, and I use one hand to cover my ears while waving toward her to quiet down.

A bright white light emanates like the sun from Sydney's mouth as her cape flies at her back while a howling wind funnels around her.

"Sydney!" I call out, not wanting to use my own dark gifts to subdue her.

But she is too far gone.

Growling, I raise my arms to my sides, summoning my shadows from the dark caves of the origin of mirth. The shadows stretch out, darkening the lair as they reach out for Sydney to hold her in place.

I feel my face contort, stretching into the hollowed being all come to fear. Still, Sydney is unmoved. She stands firm, challenging me, belting a hallowing cry all her own.

Ash and molten rock whip around us, encapsulating us in a vicious flume of darkness and shadow. I know if we continue at this pace, we'll either consume the other or risk pulling the entirety of the Netherworld into oblivion.

My mind wanders, searching for the appropriate response. Had I known Amarok would set her off, I would have disposed of him the moment his feet crossed into my courtyard.

Then, it hits me. There's only one thing, one name, capable of pulling her from her demented state.

Dropping to my knees, I yield. Forcing aside my own grimly state, I do something I've never done before. Beyond the Great Prince, I've never put someone else's needs above my own. Yet, I know, even in the darkest parts of me, she is the only thing capable of lighting up my soul.

I barely let flesh cover my mouth as I lift my head amid the whipping wind, hopeful she sees me. Not her pain. Not her fear. Just me, the Grim lord who now wears a fucking heart on a sleeve.

"Hala," I cry out, my eyes burning from the brightness she emits.

Slowly, the wind settles around us as she halts her shrieking cry.

"Hala," I repeat as I watch Syd drop to her knees in front of me.

Lifting her face to mine, the black streaks marring her cheeks pierce my heart more than she knows. "What did you say?" she whispers, almost breathless.

"I will protect Hala. I swear it."

"But my lord, if Amarok is still out there—he's more dangerous than ever! Believe it or not, it was likely Purcival who held his sway. He'll surely hunt us both."

The thought of Amarok coming within an inch of Sydney strikes an ominous chord within me, blackening my eyes. "He'll die first."

Palming her face, Sydney cries, bending at the waist. Quickly, I make my way to her side, but my shadows reach her before I can. Dark arms stretch around her, comforting her from all sides as dancing embers hover over her.

I've never seen anything as hauntingly beautiful in my entire existence.

Slowly, she lifts her head, a small smile gracing her lips, and I know this woman was made for me.

# CHAPTER 18

# *Lorna Sydney*

Tears fill my eyes as the most magnificent display of Grim magic crowds around me.

When Thelios first brought me here, I thought it was a beautiful mausoleum of sorts, but this is so much more. Every part of the place feels welcoming, kindred, even. As strange as it sounds, I feel at home here.

Perhaps it's because Thelios has welcomed me into a part of himself I'm sure he's never shown to anyone else, but even still, this place feels more comforting than anywhere in the Netherworld.

Although it pains me to know Amarok is still out there, the look in Thelios' eyes assures me I have nothing to fear.

"I'm sorry," I painfully confess.

Rushing toward me, Thelios wraps me in his arms. There's still a dusting of ash and molten rock flying around us, but neither of us seems to mind. All I need is him right now, and if I had to guess, I'm sure he feels the same.

"You have nothing to apologize for, sweetness," he adds, kissing the top of my head.

"The way I reacted, I—I could have hurt you or worse." My voice trails off into tears.

He lets out a small laugh. "I wouldn't worry about that."

I pull back a little and give him a stare. If only he could see my eyes right now. "What's that supposed to mean?" I grumble. He has no idea how hard I worked to restrain myself.

Thelios laughs once more. "It's not to say you aren't dangerous, love, but I'd wager that even if you were to remove this hood, I'd still be standing strong."

I shake my head, unconvinced. "How can you be so sure?"

Narrowing his gaze, he gives me a wink. "Let's just say I'd gamble all that I am for you, lovely. I have, too, since the moment you walked into my life."

I let out a breath I hadn't even noticed I was holding and plunge my head back into his chest. I don't think either of us is ready for that discussion yet.

Tugging my fingers along his collar, I look up at him. "I need to get to Hala. I need to make sure she's safe."

He grabs my chin. "No, love. *We* need to make sure Hala is safe." Looking down at me, there's an earnest gaze seeping from him I never thought a death-ridden grim lord like him could ever muster. Yet here he is, looking at me like he's ready to give me the world.

"Yes" I correct myself. *"We do."* The thought is refreshing, calming the frenzy brewing in my gut.

Once more, Thelios squeezes me into his chest as he plants a lingering kiss on the top of my hood. For the first time, I find myself hating this wretched cloak I must wear. It's the only thing separating me from the feel of his mouth. Still, I'll take what I can get for now. Sooner or later, however, this hood is coming off.

"We should get going," he begins, locking our arms together as he leads us to a molten stream. "We can take my ferry. We'll get there faster."

"Get where faster?" I ask, curious.

With a wave of his scythe through the air, Thelios summons his ferry, and I watch in awe as the unmanned vessel floats down the stream toward us. Thelios steps inside first, and as he does, he instantly returns to his grimly state. It happens so fast, fiery embers hovering around him, that I blink once, and he becomes the Grim lord of Purgia.

Holding his hand out toward me, I place my palm into his boney hand. It's the one thing I never thought I wanted to do—board the ferry of a Grim—but here I am.

His skeletal grin dashes at me as he gently trails his fingers down my shoulder and brings me to his side. Speaking the sacred words of his ferry, he commands it forward, and we begin moving.

"You still haven't told me where we're going," I say when the silence sits too long between us.

"Pella has Hala waiting for us at the Soleil," he quietly answers, somewhat distracted in thought.

As much as I want to know what's bothering him, I'm more curious about my sister. "What are they doing there?"

Groaning, he turns toward me with his arms folded over his chest. "Well, it was supposed to be a surprise. I wanted it to be a celebration of sorts—you know, for your freedom. Reaper was to have Pella arrange for you and your sister to dress in Purgian garb from the Soleil."

A small gasp escapes me at the thoughtful gesture. Placing my hand on his shoulder, I smile. "That's so kind of you, my lord."

Narrowing his gaze, he gives me a stern glance. "Why must you insist on formalities?"

"Maybe I'm in need of another lesson in manners," I playfully answer, biting my fingernail.

Taking my hand from my mouth, he leads me in front of him. "Keep it up, and I'll have you screaming my name all the way to the Soleil," he grunts as he grabs my backside and pushes me forward.

"You wouldn't dare," I moan, hopeful he takes me up on another dare.

Guiding my hand to his crotch, he ensures I feel the rock-hard bulge swelling through his cloak.

"Actually, you're right. I wouldn't." His eyes deepen, black and hollow, as he looks at me, but I feel like I can see into his soul. I want to linger in his gaze, but I feel my body being shoved down from the top of my head. "In fact," he continues, "I've got better uses for that mouth of yours. Lay back."

I do as he says, adjusting myself on the extra cloaks laying on the deck floor. Thelios speaks some ancient words I cannot understand, and the black sails of his ferry fly open, covering us.

Hovering over me, Thelios releases his hard length after ripping open my bodice so that my breasts spill out. As he does, my nipples instantly harden and dampen with my arousal, as does my sex. Shifting himself so he is fully straddled over me, he places his shaft between my breasts.

"Damn it, Sydney. You have no idea how long I've been waiting to fuck your pretty little mouth. Open wide for me." Eagerly, I part my lips, enjoying the feel of his cock burrowing through my cleavage and into my mouth. Growling, his skeletal grin grows wide. "We're going to have a milking, session sweetness. You nourish my dick with your milk, and I'll nourish your throat with my cum. I want us both dripping and drenched."

Gathering my breasts, he lodges his length between them. Working my nipples and squeezing my mounds, he thrusts himself back and forth into my mouth.

"That's right, my sweet Syd. Milk me. Fucking drain me," he growls, shoving more of his length down my throat.

Long, thick, and veiny, his girth jars my mouth open, making my jaw go slack as he ruts like I have no gag reflex. Thankfully for him, I don't.

He's got one hand on my neck, the other circling and squeezing my nipples as profane utterances pour from his lips as he ravages my body for his own pleasure.

"Look at you, taking me so well. I knew those pretty red lips were made to take this dick," Thelios roars as he pumps relentlessly into me.

I'm not even sure how it's possible, but he's lodged so far in the back of my throat, I feel like he's going to literally enter my windpipe. But still, I take him. I charm that venomous monster of his, sucking and coaxing him as far as I can until black tears race down my cheeks.

"That's it," he coos. "That's my good girl. Now, swallow quickly. We'll be there soon," he calls out as he jacks off into my mouth. His sweet, smoky flavor settles over my tongue, filling me with more than I can handle. "Sydney!" he roars, his hand still nestled on my throat as I gulp heap after heap of his heavy load.

"Mmm..." I moan as he slowly slips from my mouth and rolls next to me. I wipe the side of my mouth. "A little dribble," I giggle, licking my lips.

Thelios is laid out, still clutching his cock as a look of relief washes over his face.

"Did I do okay?" I ask, leaning over him. "You know, for my first time?"

"Your first time?" he exclaims, slowly sitting up. Taking my face in his hands, he looks me over like I'm a wishing star. "Sydney, you just deep throated me like I always knew you could. You have undoubtedly made my wish come true."

A bashful smile is all I give in reply. If it weren't for the looming presence of Amarok, I can honestly say that I have never been happier.

How lovely it feels holding Sydney in my arms like this.

I never thought I could have someone like her in my life. Now, here I am, hope springing like a well inside of me, telling me anything is possible.

*Perhaps even lo...*

No, idiot. Don't go there.

Too soon. At least, not until we deal with Amarok.

Sydney plants a small kiss to my chin, returning my attention to her. "Where'd you go again?" she asks with a small strum of her hand along my jawline.

I sit up, helping her with me. "Again?" I add a small smirk.

"That's the second time I've seen your eyes go distant, Thelios. You're not fooling me."

An appreciative grin covers my bone-ridden face. "Seeing as I have no eyes to speak of at the moment, I hardly think you saw *my eyes* go anywhere, sweetness." Looking down at her, I offer a playful shove, but with her mouth crumpled to one side, I know she's not buying it.

"Thelios." Sydney's deadpan tone hits me square in the throat, forcing my truth.

I let out an exasperated sigh, the kind men do when their wives ask where they've been all night. "I'm disappointed, that's all," I finally confess, strangely happy to get it off my chest.

"Oh, did I–"

Grabbing her shoulders when I see her hunch inward, I lift her chin. "No, Syd, it's not you–you've done nothing wrong. It's not us. It's not Hala or anyone else."

"Then what is it?"

"It's me! I can't believe I et Amarok escape!" I growl, jumping up from the floor.

Sydney quickly stands behind me, gently running her hand up my back. "Thelios, my lord, you can't blame yourself. That's on me. Had I told you about him aligning with Purcival from the beginning—"

Turning to face her, I shake my head in protest. "No, even that's not on you. That's on me. I've sat idly by while some LowLand magistrate scalped my own lottery. If the Great Prince hears about this upon his return–"

"His return?" Sydney mumbles, stepping back. "He's gone?"

Sucking in a breath, I take her hand in mine. "Listen, Sydney, no one is really supposed to know. Only those of us in the High Court are aware of his absence."

With her hand covering her mouth, Sydney shakes her head in understanding. "That explains it."

I frown. This can't be good. "Explains what?" My frustration doesn't go unnoticed as I watch Syd's mouth twist once again.

"Remember when I told you I saw Hala earlier today? Well, Pella had her and another girl hide near an old tunnel near the galley."

Hence why the faint stench of hydra husks seeped into her pores. "Why would Pella do that?"

"They spotted a herd of Scullards nearby."

"More Scullards?" I bark.

Sydney steps back, giving me some necessary distance. I wish I could relish in just how much this woman seems to discern my moods appropriately. It's like she really knows me. But I can't focus on that now. I've got to deal with this.

"That wretched Amarok must've known the Great Prince was gone, my lord."

"Yes, and that's why he dared show his face in court," I snarl. Then, it hits me. "That wretched Purcival must have told him the prince was gone."

Syd nods in agreement. "I think he's been planning this longer than even I've considered."

"Fucking wretch!" I snap back, but she doesn't flinch. She knows my mood isn't meant for her. When this is all said and done, I'll show her how much I appreciate her.

Taking a deep breath, I ponder my strategy. I'll have to bring Reaper in on this. We'll need almost the entirety of the dark guard to disband this herd before they descend on the whole of Purgia. Besides, I don't know what promises Hades made to Amarok, and since that sniveling Purcival is gone, who knows to what lengths he'd go.

With folded arms, I pace the length of the ferry as we near the Soleil. We'll be there in no time, so I have to consider my priorities and every facet of what this threat poses for all Purgians, even more so now that the Great Prince is gone. "Do you think Amarok will return to track down Hala?"

"Yes, and not just her, but me too."

I halt my strolling. "What?" I snarl as my head whips over my shoulder. "I thought you said he wanted Hala as a milking wench, that the bastard Purcival said you were sullied."

Sydney drops her head, a lone black tear falling to her chin. "Thelios, I–I wanted to tell you–but I was afraid—I didn't know what to do, so I took Hala and—"

A whipping flume of shadows break off into the wind at my back, only to once more return to my being as a loud, screeching roar bellows through me. "No!" I shout, nothing but flames burning my fists at my side.

Falling to the floor, Sydney curls into a ball and cries.

Nothing but rage mars my view of the perfect woman at my feet, but the thought of anyone violating her makes me want to tear Amarok's soul apart, splinter by splinter.

"I'm sorry, Thelios. I should have told you."

My shadows lull me out of my rage down to her side, wrapping my arms around her. "You don't have to relive that pain."

"But I want to explain. It wasn't me, my lord. It was Hala. When the bastard couldn't force me to feed one of his filthy beasts, he stripped Hala bare as revenge, right in front of our father, and forced her to feed him while Father watched." Sydney is a puddle of tears as she recounts what happened to Hala. Now her endless instinct to protect her sister makes much more sense. "Amarok said he was leaving to get more of his herd. Said he'd force Hala to nourish them and that he'd let the herd do what they pleased with me."

"He'll never touch you or Hala again." There's a new swell in my throat, and even the hollow cavity around my eyes feels damp.

Pulling her close, I swaddle her in my cloak. It's a strange sensation—if I didn't know better, I'd say her flesh melded off the bone just as mine has done countless times. *Strange.*

"Thank you, Thelios," she says before pulling out of my embrace and rising to her feet. Using the back of her wrist, she wipes the remaining tears from her eyes.

"You can thank me once I send that murderous leech into oblivion."

Sydney's mouth parts in shock. "You can do that? I thought folk just settled into your mirth like some lonely island."

"Not quite, but yes, I can send him and anyone else into oblivion of mirth, where his soul is repeatedly shredded as his final act of existence."

Covering her mouth, she gasps. "That sounds horrible and perfect all the same," she says, her mouth curving into a wicked grin.

We marvel in silence as we near our destination. My mind fixes a thousand different ways to end Amarok while, if I had to guess, there's only one person on Sydney's mind: Hala.

The ferry lands on the shoreside of the Soleil, and I utter the enchantment to lower my sails.

Helping Sydney out first, I climb out behind her. My body instantly returns to my fleshly state, and I can almost see the relief in Sydney's posture as I transform—although she didn't seem to mind what I looked like when she had my girth between her pretty pouty lips.

Sadly, I don't have time to linger on the thought when an echo of shouts ring out no sooner than we arrive.

"Stay close," I bark over my shoulder. Sydney affirms with a slight nod as we take one final glance at one another before racing head-on toward the grueling noises just beyond our view.

# CHAPTER 20

# Lorna Sydney

"Syd!" Hala screams as Thelios and I charge inside the red tent of the Soleil. Throwing her petite arms around my neck, she squeals so loudly, I can barely hear anything else.

Quickly pulling her from me, I examine her, surprised to find a wide smile stretching across her face. I flit my gaze around the Soleil, shocked to see the makings of celebration ringing about.

"What's going on here?" I whisper, more to Thelios than my sister.

With a tight grip on my palm, Hala shrieks with excitement, jumping up and down. "Isn't it wonderful, sister? It's just like Father always said!"

She quickly releases my hands and rushes to Thelios' side. Tossing her small arms around his waist, she squeezes him tight. Groaning, his half-painted calavera smile tells of his discomfort, but his softened expression as he stares at me shows how even Hala can wear down the Grim lord of the Netherworld.

"Father always said only the Grim lord could save us, and so you have!" she confesses.

"Did he now?" Thelios says warmly, slowly pulling out of her embrace while giving her hand a gentle squeeze. He gives me a look, likely surprised by my sister's admission, and I know he'll grill me about it once we're alone.

"Yes! Father always said–"

"Hala!" I interrupt her. I don't need her going down the rabbit hole of all the things Father used to say—at least, not right now. "Listen, sister, I've come–I mean, we've come—to take you with us. We need to go. Now."

Folding her arms at her chest, Hala frowns, her bottom lip nearly hanging to her chin. "Well aren't you a downer? I mean, look around, Syd," Hala says, waving her arms around the Soleil.

My eyes travel the wide circumference of the tent, momentarily marveling at the ornamental columns and display of fabrics hanging from the hanging rings above. There's a woman, clad in gold from head-to-toe and a rotund man at her side with gold leaves at either side of his ear, standing near the columns. I'm sure they're the stewards of the Soleil. All my life, I've dreamt of entering the sanctuary of the Soleil, to behold the array of beauty found in no part of the Netherworld save Purgia.

"I mean, you haven't even noticed my pretty dress!" Hala whines, flourishing the hem of her dress in the air. "Isn't it lovely?" There's a sweet lilt to her voice that's both disappointed at my lack of notice and excited to show me her new attire.

"Think about it Syd," she says, pulling my hand and leading me around. I try not to let the sounds of merriment and music in the background distract me. "We can finally retire our ash-ridden garb and dress like real Purgians! I mean, isn't that what we always wanted?"

Sighing, I feel bad for wanting to pull her away from here, and the smile alone on her face is melting away my defenses.

"It is beautiful, Hala," Thelios chimes in when he notices I'm at a loss for words. "And I think your new attire is lovely. In fact, I arranged this all so you and Sydney could fully assimilate into Purgian life."

"Oh! Thank you so much, my lord!" Hala squeals again, jumping up and down at my side.

"Well, yes but we must–"

"Dance!" she shouts, looping her arm through mine as the loud thump of drums and fluted instruments ring through the air.

Groaning, Thelios pulls at my opposite arm. "Syd, we mustn't linger," he grits through his teeth into my ear. I can tell he's trying to restrain himself and not go full grim-mode, but Hala is definitely challenging his resolve.

"Oh, come on, you can spare a dance," a low, grumbly voice bellows from behind.

Looking over Thelios' shoulder, my jaw drops at the sight of the hulking being now looming just behind Thelios. His broad shoulders are as wide as two Netherworld doors, and just one glance at the large scythe mounted across his shoulder tells me I've come face to face with the Reaper lord of the Netherworld.

"Reaper!" Thelios grins, shifting to stand at my side.

"Lord Grim." Reaper's gruff tone reeks of smoke as he exchanges glances between me and Thelios. "And you must be the Specter he's told me so much about. Sydney," he adds, tipping his head slightly toward me.

"My lord Reaper." I bow at the waist. "The pleasure is all mine."

Thelios steps in front me, quirking a brow down at my bustline, flecks of envy darkening his eyes. "We need to talk," he mutters matter-of-factly, turning back to Reaper.

"Fine. Let's talk. But let the women dance," Reaper grumbles back, rubbing the stubble along his jaw. "This is to be a celebration, is it not?"

"Dance, but Ro–"

A bright golden light flashes between us, halting Thelios' rebuttal.

Glittery golden wings flutter before us, making a buzzing, almost lyrical sound as a moss-hued pixie comes into view. With a bouncing purple bun and a singular horn just between two golden eyes, she flutters at Hala's side.

"Pella, do you mind?" Thelios gripes, shooing the pretty little fairy away.

"Actually I do," she frowns, her hands on her small hips as she hovers over my sister's shoulder. "You told Reaper I should carry about a proper celebration and have Hala and her sister arrayed in Purgia's finest. You told me to spare no expense!"

I gasp, covering my mouth in shock. "You did?"

A tender gaze drifts through Thelios' eyes, but I know enough to know he won't stand for such gentle displays before this crowd. "That's not the point, Pella. There are bigger things going on here–"

"Ah-hem..." Reaper clears his throat, tugging Thelios by his elbow. "You said we should talk. Leave the women to their... um... frivolities." He shoots a look toward me and Pella.

"Hmph," Pella playfully grunts as her wings flap hard at her back. Nodding at me and Hala, she gestures for us to head toward the center of the Soleil.

"Come on, Syd! Liv is waiting for us!" Hala exclaims, pointing to Liv waving at us from across the room.

I turn back to Thelios, still unsure what to do as the threat of Amarok looms in my mind. I watch as his tightened jaw grinds side to side as he's pulled away by Reaper.

Peering over his shoulder, he gives me a look. "I'll be right back." Thelios' tone is dry and quick as he's quickly led just outside the tent.

"It's okay," Pella offers, patting my shoulder. Her golden eyes glimmer, her wings fluttering at her back as she shares a comforting smile. "We'll be right here when Grim and Reaper return. I'll keep you safe. Promise." She throws me a wink.

I'm not sure how a creature so small thinks she can protect me, but I forge ahead, doing my best not to seem ungrateful for her kindness.

Even more, it's been so long since I've seen my sister this happy. Now, here she is, dancing and making friends. This is all I ever wanted for her.

"Dance with me, Syd!" Hala's voice rings loud over the sound of merriment sweeping around the Soleil. Everyone here seems so happy and jovial. I've never seen anything like it. The Netherworld is such a dark and ominous place, but Purgia has shown me why folk barter and plea to be a resident.

My eyes water at the thought. *Hala and I are now citizens of Purgia.*

Short moments pass, and I'm hand in hand with Hala as we sway in step with the music. In her lovely new shimmering silver cloak and lilac dress, my sister twirls around me, stomping her feet in rhythm with the drums. I can't recall the last time either of us danced, or even had reason to, but now seems like an appropriate time.

But when the crashing sound of breaking glass shatters around us, the festive tone of the Soleil comes to a screeching halt.

Then comes the screams—loud, menacing roaring sounds, and I watch in horror as large, snarling beasts barrel through the tent doors.

"Sydney!" Hala screams as I pull her aside while a huge Scullard bores its tusks toward us.

Pella releases a high-pitched cry as her wings grow wider, and she fires her pixie dust into the creature's eyes, blinding it. "That'll hold 'em," she huffs, turning toward us. "Stay close." She gives me a nod.

Another Scullard plows through the entrance, and I give my sister a look. I don't know where either the Grim or Reaper lords are, but I know one thing: we are Specters. We can save ourselves. Tearing back our hoods, we release a suspension of hell so strong, we keep the beasts at bay.

"Send the guard around the perimeter! I'll head inside!" I shout over my shoulder to Roark as he plows his blade through another mangy beast.

Scullards are precisely what they are, disheveled wolf-like creatures who hunt flesh, both living and dead, to survive. They are as vile as they are grotesque, with thick, long tusks exuding from their underbites and razor sharp teeth. It's no wonder Sydney fears the harm they could cause to her and Hala.

I won't allow it.

Rushing back into the tent, my eyes quickly scan the room. I still don't see Amarok. Thankful to see Sydney is safe, I'm impressed by how she and Hala are holding back a few of the horde with just their hellish glare. Dark, shadowy light bores through the two sisters as the creatures cower at the sound of their call.

Plugging their ears and clawing themselves, the Scullards quake with fear as Sydney and Hala fight them off. Pella and Liv are splattering fairy dust around the perimeter, just enough to keep any other Scullards from coming too close. My admiration of the women's feat is short-lived, though, when I'm hit from behind by Amarok.

"Bastard of Mirth!" he snarls, spitting to the ground at my side. "You may have sunk Purcival into your grime, but you'll find me far more difficult," he says, shoving his hoof into my sternum.

Grinding my teeth, I merely wince at the pain when my familiars slither out from under the sleeves of my cloak and tear into Amarok's heel.

Howling, he falters to the side as En Cala and En Serif's venom sears his flesh. Swiping him with the side of my scythe, I knock him to the ground as my shadows lift me from the floor. Towering over him, I jab the blunt end of my rod into his abdomen.

Amarok's eyes are laden with fear, but I see he'll not relinquish defeat. "After them!" he shouts to another brood flooding through the door, pointing at Sydney and Hala. "Ahh… and the pixie!" he snarls, his gaze staring straight at Pella.

Ramming my foot into his jaw, I issue a bellowing roar of ash and soot that knocks him out cold. I want to end him, take my time to pull his soul apart bit by bit, but right now, I have to stop the herd closing in around the women.

"Pella!" I shout, and she turns toward me. I want to call for Sydney, but with she and Hala uncloaked, I don't want to get caught in their hallowing glare. "Get them out of here!" Casting my scythe in their direction, I open a portal to Kilgo Falls. As a resident fae in the realm of the High Serpent Queen, I know Liv can keep them safe until we get this herd under control.

"Pixies!" one of the beasts shouts, calling after Pella and Liv.

Liv throws a mound of dust toward them, temporarily blinding a few Scullard in her reach.

"Go now!" I order, and Pella nods at me with understanding.

"Hala! Sydney!" I shout at their backs as I see their defenses slightly waning. Hala limps, but Liv catches her and pulls her into the portal. "Go, Sydney! Get your sister out of here!" I call out, but Syd tosses her hood back on and briefly turns to me.

As she does, she is pulled from behind by the beast from before. "Get the ring!" he commands another creature.

"Sydney!" Hala screams as she reaches for her sister, but Liv pulls her back. "Sister!" she cries, removing her hood, blasting one of the beasts with her glare, using the last of her strength.

The first Scullard snatches the ring from around Sydney's neck as he smacks her to the ground, and Pella shrieks, hurling a wind of fiery dust at the creature, allowing Sydney to pry the ring from its mangy claws.

"No, Sydney!" I cry out, fearful when I see the ring slip onto her finger. Having the ring on a cord around her neck is one thing, but I fear the deadly consequence of a non-grim wearing it properly. I lose my will to keep the portal open as I rush to her, but the feel of a sharp blade at my back tumbles me to the floor.

"The Bastard of Mirth finally on his knees!" Amarok sneers, licking my blood from his knife as he stands over me. "Now we know a Grim can bleed. Better test out another theory," he roars, lifting his arm to strike me.

As he does, I see Sydney through the gap under his reach. "Amarok!" she roars as she rips off her hood.

For a brief moment, I see her.

She's the most beautiful creature, with long, thick, raven black hair, skin pale as moonlight, and eyes blazing bright like brimstone. Lorna Sydney alone personifies perfection in every way.

Then, I see it.

Dark lines thread beneath her skin, tethering the calavera skull texture to one side of her face as the opposite hollows into nothingness, just as mine has done countless times before.

*Impossible!*

My grave ridden heart sinks to the floor as the revelation becomes clear.

Sydney is a Grim.

Or at least partly, as she still manages to bellow a Specter wail, hurling Amarok to the floor at my side. Motioning her arm around, she forms a chasm all her own that splinters him like wheat as it pulls him into her murky flume.

Nothing but the clanking sound of his blade hitting the ground is all I hear as he is swallowed into Sydney's mirth.

But that could only mean...

"Thelios!" she cries, hurrying toward me as tears race down her face.

Crab walking away from her, I lift my hand in caution. "Stay away from me!" I shout.

Wiping her eyes, she frowns, dropping to my side. "Thelios, I–"

Jumping up from the floor, I feel my own shadows retreat within me as a cold tingle prickles my spine. "How could you?" I bite, swiping my hand hard through the air.

Shaking her head, Sydney takes cautious steps toward me. "I–I don't know how any of this is possible, but–"

"But nothing! You are a Grim! That's why you have the ring. Was this your sick plan all along? To lure me—"

"Lure you?" she protests, her eyes hollowing out once more.

I swallow hard. "What is it that you want, Sydney? To cover the world in shadow? To bring about oblivion?"

Growling, Sydney balls her fists at her sides, doing what she can to resist her own grim state from taking over. "Thelios, please, I love—"

Roaring, a gust of wind funnels around me. "Don't you dare speak such words to me, you wretch! I haven't the faintest what sort you are, you—you Specter, but Grim kind doesn't lay with Grim-kind. It is an abomination!"

"Thelios, please, I–"

"Enough words!" I growl, my shadows stretching out from my sides, causing me to tower over Sydney. "You may be a Grim, but there is still only one Grim Lord!"

"My lord!" Sydney cries, dropping to her knees.

Once more, I feel dampness at the hollowing of my own eyes, but I have no tears to cry. A part of me wishes I could, if only to blur the vision of the woman to whom I'd hoped to give my all.

For the first time in my existence, I felt love and was loved, or so I thought. Surely, this cannot be love. One cannot love his own kin in this manner. It is blasphemy. Forbidden. Wrong.

Slowly, Sydney lifts her face to me, and I see her as I did the first time I laid eyes on her: a lovely, dark flower, crushed, bruised, and broken. Everything in me wants to pull her in my arms and cover her in the shadow of my love and drown in the perfume of her brokenness.

I'd let the world burn. Fall into shadow. Blow into fucking oblivion. Anything. As long as I can make her mine.

But I cannot.

I am not simply a man who can bear his heart on a whim.

I am not a man, and I have no heart.

So, I do what only a true heartless monster like me can do: swallow her into my mirth.

# TALES OF

## ROARK

Species- Reaper Lord & Death Dealer

Powers- Master Scythe Wielding, Soul Separating, Impermeable Strength

# REAPER

## PELLA

Species- Pixie/Sprite

Powers- Light magic, hallucinations, pixie dust

CHAPTER 22

*Roark*

Rushing inside, nothing but a whipping wind of ash and soot skirt around the Soleil.

The sound of screams tinged with the remnants of defeat loom as the Scullards race about, retreating from all sides.

It's the sight of Thelios now crumpled to the floor stopping me in my tracks.

"Thelios!" I grunt, kicking him in the side, hoping to pull him out of his daze. Meanwhile, I scan the perimeter, only to find withered carcasses arrayed around the once ornamental center of Purgia. "Thelios!" I groan once more, and this time he moves just enough to evade my boot.

Pained, dark, glassy eyes look up at me with an expression I've never seen before on the Grim lord of the Netherworld.

"Where are the women?" I ask as he slowly claws his way up from the ground, using his scythe as leverage. With black tar stains covering the floor, I have no doubt Thelios has either sent many to his mirth or opened a portal.

"What?" he says, brushing the dust from his gown as he stands upright.

I step in front of him, surprised to find one lone tear sitting like a black diamond on his cheekbone. I can only wonder what really happened here.

"The women," I repeat, looking away, as if I don't notice him wiping his face. "Where are they?"

"How would I know?" he grumbles, adjusting the hook on his scythe.

Grumbling, I kick a disheveled Scullard husk aside. "For fuck's sake, Thelios! I don't know what's going on with you, but–"

"My lords!" The sound of Gao, Chief Steward of the Soleil, shouting from the side entrance calls my attention. "Hurry!"

Giving a quick look to Thelios, I do my best to shake off whatever is going on with him. Thelios takes off before me, and I follow, heading toward Gao.

"My lords, Grim, Reaper–they have her!" Gao shrieks, pointing at a caravan of Scullards heading west.

"Who?" Thelios asks.

"Pella, my lords!" Gao yelps, rubbing his balding head. "Oru and I tried, but they knocked her out," he says, gesturing to his wife, now propped against the tent wall.

"Shit!" I growl. "You were supposed to keep the women safe!" I snap over my shoulder to Thelios. "Do they have all of them?" I say to Gao.

Shrugging his shoulders, he looks down at his wife.

"No," she manages, holding herself at the waist. "Liv and the little Specter went through the portal," she adds, pointing to Thelios.

Huffing, I look at him. "Well, why didn't you just say that? And the eldest sister?"

Thelios' jaw tightens, and his eyes darken as he looks at me.

Now, it all makes sense. He lost her.

Placing my hand on his shoulder, I give it a squeeze. "I'm sorry, my lord Grim."

Narrowing his gaze, Thelios parts his mouth to say something, but he pushes the thought aside. Shifting so that my hand is no longer on him, he manages a sigh. "We need to get Pella."

"What could the Scullard filth want with a sprite?" I scratch my jaw with the corner of my blade.

Gao helps his wife to stand, and she winces a bit. "Why, my lord, Pella is the last of the Viridian Sprites. Pixie blood such as hers is quite valuable to Scullards. That's why the Great Prince rarely lets her out. He knew if they knew of her existence–"

"Damn it!" I smash my fist through an adjacent tent pole, and Gao grimaces as I do, likely annoyed, especially with the Soleil in such a disarray as it is.

"My lord," Oru continues. "The Scullard herd only runs for yet another night watch. You'll need to get Pella and keep her safe until then. Hopefully, the Great Prince would have returned before that time."

"Fine. The Grim lord and I can get her and bring her back–"

"No, my lord!" Gao adds. "I don't think Purgia could survive another Scullard attack, especially not so close to Festivus. You need to take her far from here."

"Where can we take her?" Thelios asks, sharing a wary glance with me.

"No, Thelios," I begin, patting his back. "I'll get her. You stay."

"Reaper, please," he protests, pulling away from me. "There's no way I'll let you fight the Scullard filth all on your own."

Folding my arms, I raise a brow, lifting my chin just slightly over my shoulder as I tilt my head to the forming guard at my rear. "I won't be alone," I smirk.

His posture relaxes as he looks behind me at the dark guard. "But–"

"But nothing, my lord Grim," I counter. "I'll take care of retrieving the prince's ward. He'll give us shit or have our heads if he returns and she's missing or worse."

Thelios nods in agreement. "Indeed."

"Besides, my lord," Oru adds in a softer tone, "Festivus is quickly approaching. We'll need your aid in assuring all the preparations."

"Usque ad mortem!" I roar over my shoulder to the guard.

"Onward to death!" they rally in return.

Throwing my scythe over my shoulder and heaving my ax into my halter, I turn towards the dark guard as we head toward the city gates.

"Roark!" Thelios shouts, halting me before I take my leave. As I turn around, I'm surprised at how close he is. "Listen, old friend: be careful. I know Pella is the ward of the Great Prince, but don't let that fool you. She's a woman." He pauses, looking at me as if that statement alone provided enough context. "I'll just say, they all have their ways. Just mind your wits," he says after throwing me a hard wink.

Shaking my head, I laugh, patting my fellow death-dealer on the shoulder. "Will someone get this man a drink?" I call out toward Gao and Oru as Thelios slowly walks away. I can only hope a stiff drink relieves him of his grief.

"E*xcresco!*" the large, mole-ridden Scullard snarls, banging on the glass jar.

I barely saw Liv pull Hala through the portal before I was grabbed from behind and thrown into this glass prison.

Scullards and men alike have an affinity for capturing glowing beings like my kind, even my firefly cousins of the earth realm. Mortals think it's a cute child's trick to light jars filled with luminous creatures, thinking nothing of the fatal pain we endure. Scullard Beasts care only about using our mortality against us in effort to trick us into growing larger.

I'd rather die first.

I would rather suffocate in this glass sarcophagus than reveal my true form. I'm no fool. I know the Scullards want to force me to grow into a larger size so they can use my body for their own depraved pleasures. Even worse, they want me to bear their wretched offspring.

I won't give them the satisfaction.

"Excresco!" the filthy Scullard shouts again. This time, he pounds the top of the glass so hard, the loud sound makes me dizzy, and I grab my ears as I fall to the bottom of the jar. "Maybe not now, but you *will* grow for me, little pixie!"

Balling into a knot, I crowd my knees to my chin, flapping my wings to relieve me of this dizzying feeling.

*No one is coming for you*, fear calls to me, but I'll not hear it. My heart reaches to the darkness, shrouding me like a shadow, and in a private moment, I pour out my soul. *Help will come*, I console myself.

Still, with the Great Prince, Kharon, the Ferryman, away on the earthbound realm, neither Grim nor Reaper even noticed my disappearance. Not that either of them have ever really seen me as anything but a meddling fly who happens to be the prince's ward, but still, the thought is painful to ponder. Shaking my head, I repeat my call into the Night. Help will come. I know it.

My entire family, the Sprites of Viridian, were mutilated by Scullards some time ago. That's when Prince Kharon took me in. I was the only one able to flee from their vicious tyranny.

In fact, until now, the Scullards likely believed none survived.

That is, until they saw me at the Soleil.

The prince rarely lets me leave the halls of his High Court, much less wander about Purgia. He knows the peril I face if I am seen. But it has been more night watches than I can count since I ventured outside of the palace walls, and even then, I was securely nestled within the prince's reach.

Of course, Fate plots against me. On my first occasion outside of the palace, I'm not only spotted by Scullards, but taken captive. There'll be hell to pay when the Great Prince returns.

"Riza!" a smaller Scullard snarls, hunched over as he walks under the tented tree line.

"What is it?" Riza growls back, looking at his map under a small lamp.

"We've checked the perimeter. Scouts haven't seen any movement from the east."

Laughing, Riza turns to look at me inside the jar on the wagon. "You hear that, little sprite? No one's coming to save you. Best you start playing nice." Drool drips from his tusks as he watches me, and he licks his lips as darkness dances behind his eyes.

"Mmm... She looks like she can serve our needs well, General," the smaller Scullard groans, rubbing his hands together as he ambles close to the wagon.

"Back off, Findrell!" Riza growls, shoving my jar to the corner of the wagon. "Now that Amarok's gone, I'm in charge, and no one's touching pixie booty before me."

Findrell skulks back, his sunken eyes still peering at me over Riza's large, hairy shoulders. Tipping his head, he makes his way back to the camp horde.

"You see, little sprite? I saved you this time. I can't promise that'll happen again," he says, chugging back a heap of barley wine. Tapping on the glass with his thick, furry forefinger, his lips contort into the most disgusting smile I've ever seen. "But if you don't grow, little one, I'll have to add the cap. I'd hate to watch a pretty little pixie like you suffocate, but if that's how you want it–"

Turning away from Riza, I fold my arms and face the corner of the wagon. I'll not give him the decency of my voice. If he wants to kill me, so be it.

"That is," he grunts, grabbing the jar so hard I fall to the side. Laughing as he watches me tumble inside, he flips the jar so that it lands flat on his palm. "After I pluck your wings, stem by stem. It's how I got this fine trinket, after all," he sneers, running his fingers over a necklace made of pixie wings arrayed around his neck.

My eyes grow wide in shock, and I crash my fists against the glass, sending crackling lightworks throughout the jar.

Riza bellows a maddening cackle, drooling as he delights in my torment. Rolling the jar back onto the wagon, he continues laughing as he shuffles away.

Only two beasts remain guarding the wagon. While I'm thankful they're paying little attention to me, I'm disgusted by the sloppy sounds of them feasting on some nocturnal creatures they captured once they made camp.

"So I guess Riza's in charge now, huh?" one of the guards says.

"Ha!" the other scoffs, taking a big bite of what looks like an arm. "We'll see how long it lasts. He's big and bad, but he's no Amarok. Hell, if Tobin were here, there'd be no contest."

"Damn right!" the first one laughs. "Amarok and Tobin had that fool Purcival actually believe he was working for Hades."

"Idiot! As if Hades would even think of trading with the likes of us," he snorts, shaking his head.

Throwing back a large gulp of barley wine, the guards continue laughing, and as the two talk, I feel the wagon shake a little. Strange, since neither have touched either the jar or the wagon. I look around and notice the tops of trees are shaking slightly from afar. I can only hope it's what I think it is, but I do what I can to avoid bringing any attention to it.

"Well, if Amarok had gotten that Grim ring from that milking wench, then maybe he'd have something of worth to get Hades' attention."

Spitting what looks like a bone to the ground, the other Scullard picks at his fangs. "Now that's all gone to shit."

"Oh, Nethers no, mate. Not completely," he grunts as they both turn to look at me. "I'd much rather fuck a pixie. I hear there's nothing like it."

The thought sickens me, but I choose to use it to my advantage.

Once more, I feel the wagon shake, this time harder than before. One of the guards looks around, his eyes flitting up to the trees first, but I rattle around in the jar to avert his attention.

"Looky-here," the other guard coos, tapping his pointy claw against the glass. "I think she wants to play nice."

A long, slimy tongue slithers over the taller guard's tusks as he rubs his jaw. "I don't know, mate. Didn't Riza tell Findrell she was to be his first?"

The stouter guard leans over and stares into the jar, and I decide to give him a show. Leaning over just enough to show him my cleavage, his greedy gaze darts to my breasts first, then my rear, as I let my wings flutter up.

"Perhaps," he groans, lust dancing in his eyes as he watches me. Pressing myself against the glass, I ensure he gets an ample view of my bustline. "But we all know it's the first to claim an heir who gets to lead."

The taller guard steps beside him, leaning down to look at me. "Just promise me something," he whispers, still twirling a bone at the side of his mouth. The other guard gives him a knowing look. "Make sure I get a go. I don't give a damn about an heir; I just need to knock these rocks off."

Bumping shoulders, the two Scullards smile wide.

"Now look, love," the stout one begins, taking one final look over his shoulder. "I'm gonna let you out, nice and slow."

"No tricks!" the taller one grumbles as he slowly removes the vented cap.

The other beast lifts me by one of my wings as I bat my eyes, squeezing my breasts together as he holds me in his palm. I feel the wagon shake once more, and the leaves around the trees scatter into the wind.

As I gyrate seductively inside his grimy grip, their attention is so fixed on me, they have no idea what's about to come next.

Staring through the dense tree line, I'm surprised to find Pella dancing in the palms of a Scullard.

*The way she is moving...*

I've never seen Pella move like this before. Alluring. Seductive. Enchanting. A knot wells in my throat as I wonder why she would do such a thing. Maybe they've done something to her? Or perhaps she thinks this is now her lot.

I haven't the faintest idea why Pella would give in to the drooling gaze of these wretched beasts. Even more, something new stirs inside me. Envy, perhaps. I don't know. All I know is I don't like the way they're looking at her. There's a mixture of hunger and lust in their eyes, and it sickens me.

Whatever it is, it ends now.

"Excresco!" the hairy, rotund beast shrieks, salivating at the sight of Pella grinding against his furry palm.

"As you wish," she says with a cunning smirk as her wings flutter hard against her back.

Just then, a bright green light shoots through the darkened forest, and Pella grows almost to the size of a petite mortal.

"Hold her down!" a lankier one orders as he goes to grab Pella's arm, but his hands go straight through her as though she were a phantom.

"Fucking pixie magic!" the shorter beast yells as he goes to grab her once more.

*Fucking pixie magic, indeed.* He's right. I've never seen Pella this size before.

Blowing a heap of gold pixie dust, Pella blinds both Scullards and they crumple to their waists, screaming at the pain.

Damn, I think to myself. Pella doesn't need saving. An appreciative smirk spreads across my face as I watch her send another round of dusting to hold them in place. I don't have long to ogle at her stout-hearted feat when a larger Scullard plows between the others, reaching out for Pella.

"You fools!" he roars, his hands sifting through Pella's new shadowy form.

I won't let him touch her.

Growling, I strike the blade of my scythe through the tree line, tearing the branches from their limbs. A thick trunk falls first, hitting the taller one in the head, knocking him out cold.

"Happy to see me?" I wink, throwing Pella a jaunty grin.

Her eyes dance, smiling as she stares at me. "Well, I whispered to the darkness, and it sent me you." For a moment, time freezes, and all I see is her. A strange feeling wells within me that I cannot shake, but even if I could, I wouldn't.

"You're mine!" one of the beastsScullard shouts, this time capturing Pella's smaller form I hadn't noticed was just behind her phantom.

"No!" Pella squeals, working hard to get out of his clutch.

"Let her go!" I demand, banging my scythe hard against the ground. As I do, my body instantly transforms into the gangly, grotesque features most in the Netherworld have come to fear.

The shorter beast runs off, making his way toward the camp filled with the Scullard herd. Little does he know, he won't get far. My dark guard has this place surrounded.

"You don't frighten me, Reaper," the Scullard sneers, keeping a tight grip on Pella. "The pixie is mine!"

"Release her, or–"

"Or what?" he barks back. "We're outside of the province of Purgia. You have no power in the Savage Lands."

A low rumble burns through my chest at his words. The fact he believes my powers limited to Purgia shows just how little he understands of Reapers like me.

Even more, I am no mere Reaper.

I am a Reaper Lord.

Hurling my scythe through the wind, I watch as the blade wafts by Pella. Her eyes grow wide as she leans her head back, fearing the edge of my blade, but she needn't worry. Every stroke I yield is precise.

Tugging the scythe around the creature, it pierces his back, shattering his spine. His balance falters, and his grip loosens just enough for Pella to backpedal out of his hold.

The Scullard's eyes shoot up to the black sky, nothing but the whites showing as I tear him in two. Tugging hard, I rip his soul from his body in one fluid motion.

"Ahh..." he moans, struggling to speak. "I told you, Reaper: you have no power here," he foolishly cackles.

Nudging me in the shoulder, Pella gives me a look as she buzzes at my side. "But–"

Raising my palm, an all-knowing grin crowds the side of my face. "Wait for it," I say, motioning with my head for her to look down.

The Scullard's eyes follow mine, and he releases a piercing shriek at the sight of his own body now torn in half, laying on the ground.

"No!" he shrieks as the revelation of it all becomes clear. Spitting on the ground just shy of his carcass, I whip one final blow through his ghastly soul.

"Nada Pero Muerte!" I roar, banging my scythe hard against my chest.

Pella flutters low, hovering just above the Scullard's ashen husk.

"Nothing but death," she repeats, blowing what looks like black dust overtop his remains.

"What are you doing?" I groan, not keen on anyone mishandling my kill.

Pella's glowing eyes pop up to mine, and she gives me a look that lets me know I should back off. For now, I'll do just that. She was the one in peril after all. I, of all folk, can appreciate the need to claim a kill.

Even if she didn't kill him, I did it for her.

And something tells me, I'd do it again.

"We should get going," Roark barks over his shoulder, rolling his scythe through the taller Scullard finally awakening from his hit with the log. "I'll gather the guard," he says, lifting his garnet whistle to his mouth.

Rushing toward him, I swipe his hand downward. "No!"

Releasing a growl, Roark's eyes darken. "I allowed you to sully my kill. Do not think being the ward of the Great Prince allows you to challenge me."

He goes to lift the whistle to his mouth once more, and I push it down again. "Reaper, no, please!" I groan, balancing myself on his large forefinger. "I don't mean to challenge you. It's just not much of an escape if the entire horde can hear."

Roark's hulking shoulders roll in amusement. "Ah, I see. Well, it's a garnet whistle, Pella. It's silent to most. Only the guard can hear it."

"It's not the whistle that worries me," I say, now resting on his forearm. Using my magic earlier required more strength than I'm accustomed to.

He frowns, raising a brow. "Then what is it?"

"For starters, you and your guard were quite loud. I could hear you from miles around."

Once more, Roark frowns, but I can tell he is at least giving my words some thought. "You're exaggerating."

I roll my eyes. "Sadly, for your sake, I'm not."

Another Scullard pops up from behind, but Roark quickly reaches over his shoulder, striking it with a deathly blow. "Now he was loud, and now he's dead."

I feign a smile. "Are you done patting yourself on the back, Master Reaper?"

Lowering his head so our eyes meet, he growls. I'm not sure if he's trying to frighten me with his half-skeleton-half-flesh face, but I'm not scared. This isn't my first time seeing him in full view.

"Only if you're done telling me how to lead my guard." Winking at me, his mouth curves into a full skeletal grin.

"Have at it," I say, throwing him another hard eye roll. I'm too tired to argue any further.

Groaning, his mouth crumples a bit like he wants to say something, but he decides against it. "Giving up so fast?" Roark says as he swipes his blade through the trees until we reach a clearing.

"Holding a mirage like that requires a lot of strength. I'm tired."

Lifting his forearm so I'm once more eye level with him, he looks me over. "That was pretty gutsy, what you did back there."

The appreciative grin now spread across his face warms something strange inside of me. Normally, the Reaper pays me very little attention. Now that I have it, a small part of me wants to do all I can to keep him looking at me as he does now.

"Oh, it's just a little pixie magic," I smile, shrugging my shoulders.

"I don't give out compliments charitably, Pella. I meant it—you did well."

I give him a little nod. "Thank you, my lord."

"Please," he sneers, frowning a bit. "We're way past formalities. You may call me Roark."

I giggle. He always seemed so by-the-book; I never thought he'd be so relaxed with me.

"Well, okay. Roark," I say, forcing a hard R in his name. "So, how long will we need to wait? We should really get going."

Narrowing his eyes, he nods in agreement as he scans the area. "You're right—we should get a move on." Scratching his stubble, he watches me as I climb up his arm to sit on his shoulder. "Comfortable?" he grunts, sounding slightly irritated.

"Much better view from here," I chuckle, making myself comfortable along the muscular indentations between his neck and shoulder.

Groaning, he straightens his mouth into a hard line. "Don't fidget," he growls over his shoulder, still looking out into the field. "So," he begins, his voice a bit calmer. "You heard us coming?"

Everything in me wants to tease him, make him admit I was right, but, thankfully for him, I'm too tired to give him hell. "Well, believe it or not, I can hear better than most. I suppose it's a built-in survival tactic of sorts. But yes, I could hear you."

"What about the Scullards? They didn't seem to notice."

I let out a giggle. "That's because I was occupying their attention, as it were."

He swallows hard, and I watch the knot in his throat bob a few times before he manages to turn back to me. "Yeah, about that–" He can barely finish his sentiment when six members of his guard appear like a flash of smoke before us.

"Have you dispatched the feigns?" Roark asks.

The guard breathes a reply, but nothing but soot and ash seep through their iron masks. There's a small nod shared between the guards as they continue speaking, but I can't make out anything. Outside of the Great Prince himself, Reaper is the only other in the Netherworld capable of speaking the language of death.

"You should tell them that we'll split up," I whisper in his ear. Roark gives me a look, still frowning but also pondering, so I decide to continue. "The Scullards can chase after your footmen while we make our getaway back to Purgia."

"No," Roark grunts, shaking his head. "We cannot go back to Purgia, not this close to Festivus. They'll be after you."

He's right. Now that the wretched ones know of my existence, they'll never stop hunting me. "Viridia!" I exclaim as inspiration strikes.

Roark's brows lift in surprise. "What? I thought it was all but destroyed."

The thought punches me in the gut, but I choose to ignore it. "Yes, but only its inhabitants, I'm afraid. Besides, I could use the sacred land of my people to restore my strength."

Still scratching his stubble, he shifts his gaze between me and the few guards before us. "Very well then. To Viridia, we go!"

"This is the best route, I promise," Pella assures me, fluttering ahead with seemingly newfound strength.

A hum is the only acceptable answer I can muster. How I've let this little pixie give me orders is beyond me. In fact, it's not like me at all, but I can't help it. As strange as it sounds, when she speaks, I actually find myself listening. This is not my normal practice when it comes to women.

In most cases, they're brought to my lair to fulfill my carnal needs and then sent away just as quickly. It's been ages since I desired the company of a woman. The Great Prince sent a few of his harem my way upon his departure, but I sent them to the local confectionery and haven't looked for them since. I figured they were better off learning the trade of making sweet treats for the palace than sitting around my lair, waiting for a romp with me.

Besides with the size of my girth alone, I nearly killed the last woman I was with. I'm larger than most Nether folk, and that makes being with someone in that manner painfully difficult for them and frustrating for me.

Honestly, I've decided that such arrangements are frivolous at best. We are Nether. There are no love stories to be told or true love's kisses to be shared. We only have one thing to look forward to: death. As a resident death dealer, I take great pride in dealing it daily to all who are in need.

"The Midas Mountains are up ahead!" Pella's sing-song voice rings out, yanking me from my musing. Pointing to a series of gold-capped mountains along the Titan Lake, she turns to me and smiles. "Aren't they beautiful?" she coos, her eyes bright with amazement.

I only nod in agreement; I like seeing her happy.

"They're mountains alright," I grumble, not quite understanding the fascination. My foot slips on a rock, and I groan, still not completely sold on the route Pella suggested. "Shit!" I growl, kicking the rock aside as I make my way through a narrow corridor. "It's tight!"

Pella pokes out her bottom lip as she looks at me trying to squeeze through. "I'm sorry, Roark. That's another reason why I didn't think the guard should come this way. It's rather difficult to navigate."

Using my elbows, I hit the sides of the mountain until I find a break to fit in. I'm finally able to adjust enough to get through the narrow space, but I grimace when I notice that the same pattern continues for miles.

"I'll never make it through here," I say, banging my fists along the rocky wall.

Frowning, Pella pinches her chin as she looks me over. "We could try something."

"What?" I don't particularly like the look she's giving me, her eyes alive with mischief.

"But you'd have to trust me," she says, her hands now locked together under her jaw.

Gritting my teeth, I wince at the feel of the rocks tearing through my flesh. "Fine! What is it?"

"After, I'll be quite out of it, so I'll need your help."

"Just do it already!" I growl as I see rocks from above tumbling down toward us.

The words are barely out of my mouth when I feel a tingly sensation erupt all over me. Sparkling, crackling noises like fireworks burst around me, and I feel my weight lessen as my entire body glows like a shooting star.

"No time to waste!" Pella squeals with a brightened tone. I notice she doesn't sound like her usual buzzing bee self—I can hear her voice outright. Tugging my hand, I'm surprised when I feel her palm firmly pressed in mine.

"Impossible!" I shriek, marveling at the sight of Pella in full view. Usually, she looks like a small firefly. Now, however, her size is comparable to my own.

Then again...

I look down at my feet and notice they're no longer touching the ground. I'm hovering, encapsulated by a glowing orb, but it's not just that. I'm small—so much smaller than normal.

"Pella!" I growl, finally realizing she somehow shrunk me to her size.

"Oh, come on!" she laughs. "We've got a little ways to go, and I don't know how long I can hold you."

"You'll pay dearly for this!" I snarl, watching her amusement as she tugs me along the mountainous corridor.

The rocks look like boulders falling from the sky as Pella weaves us through the narrow path. She's quick and strong, pulling me as though I were a bale of hay, her shimmering golden wings fluttering rapidly at her back.

"Almost there," she says over her shoulder.

I take special notice of how her moss-hued skin is dusted with what looks like gold and diamonds. Her lofty violet bun bounces as the curly tendrils on her sides sway in the breeze she creates as she moves us along.

Until now, I've never really noticed how enchanting a creature she is.

There's a break of light ahead, letting me know we're not far from our exit, but I feel Pella's momentum slowing some.

"Pella?" I say her name, but she doesn't immediately respond.

"Almost..." she begins, turning her head slightly, but it falls to her shoulder, and so do we.

"Pella!" I shout as we plummet to the ground.

The glowing orb surrounding me slowly fades as Pella's limp body falls, face first, toward the gravel-ridden road. Large rocks fall around us, and I open my hands, hopeful to catch her.

A windfall of soot erupts from me as I hit the ground, returning to my normal stature. Reaching out my hands, Pella lands in my grip. Rolling quickly, I tumble out just before we're hit.

She's light as a feather as I stare down at the tiny creature now resting in my palms. Looking at Pella, I see her differently than before. While she still resembles a small firefly, it's clear to me now that, besides the glowing wings, the two have no similarities at all. She is not an insect.

Pella is a woman, albeit a small one, but she is a woman in every way. From the curve of her hips, to her perky bosom nestled behind the leaves that adorn her, she is an adorable sight to behold.

Slowly, her wings fold over her as she curls into the groove of my hand and rests. As I press her firmly against my chest, something new stirs inside me that I want to explore.

Nothing but the smell of rawhide leather implodes my senses as I awake from my slumber.

"Where–where am I?" My groggy tone seems to only warrant a grunt from Roark as I rub my eyes, trying to make out my surroundings. I'm tucked in a tight fit as I squirm around, still trying to get my bearings.

"Hold still," Roark's throaty voice rings over me.

I look up, only to see the bottom of his chin hairs. That's good to know. Not that I mind him in full Reaper-mode, but I'd much rather see Roark's flesh-toned features: bronzed skin, thick dark hair, and a massive, muscular frame. Roark, the Reaper lord of Purgia, is indeed very kind on the eyes. Still, I continue gazing over my shoulder until I make out a familiar set of strappings along his chest.

"You put me in your pocket!" I shriek once I'm finally able to wiggle my way out.

"You're incorrigible, you know that?" he fusses, twirling a stick around a fire. "A simple thank you would have sufficed."

"Oh, so I should be thankful to be treated as a rag you stuff in your pocket?"

"No, but you should be grateful I got us out in time before the rocks crushed us. I doubt you want your end to be so insignificant, being squashed like a—"

"To be squashed like a bug! Are you calling me an insect?"

Huffing, he shakes his head. "Those words never left my mouth."

"Only because—"

He points the fiery stick at me. "I would never call you a bug!" Roark shouts, shooting me a stern stare. "I was going to say squashed like a vine of grapes."

Folding my arms, I let out a heavy sigh, blowing a few loose tendrils from my face. "Like that's any better," I say, rolling my eyes.

"Well, squashed grapes make for good wine," he smiles, picking off a freshly roasted pine nut. "Hungry?" he grumbles, handing me a nut.

My stomach grumbles at the smell of the food, and I flutter to his side. "Maybe a little," I mumble.

Roark blows the fire off a fresh stick of roasted pine nuts and places it in his pocket. It's a thoughtful gesture; I'm sure he knows it'll be easier for me to nibble on the food this way.

"Thank you," I say after taking the first bite.

"You're quite welcome," he adds, shaking a handful of nuts into his mouth.

"You know, I'm not a big fan of grape wine."

He grunts, looking down at me with a quirked brow. "It wasn't a dig on your size, you know–"

I giggle, shaking my head. "No, no, that's not what I meant," I protest, waving a hand. "I meant literally: grape wine is kind of meh to me."

"Meh?" He frowns. "What's meh? I don't even know that word."

Smiling, I flutter up so I can see his face in full. "Oh, I'm sorry," I laugh. "It's a human term. Kora–the vampire who came recently from the earthbound plane–taught it to me. Anyway–"

"You're friends with Kora? Since when?" A dark scowl grows on his face that surprises me.

"Huh? Oh, everyone talks with Kora. I mean, he has so many stories about the earthbound realm and his dealings with mortals. His stories are rather interesting."

"I bet," Roark huffs, piercing the stick through a few more pine nuts. "Anyway," he waves his hand around, "what were you saying about the wine?"

His tone surprises me. If I didn't know better, I'd say Roark almost sounded jealous. Then again, *that's a ridiculous thought!* The Reaper lord of Purgia doesn't need to be jealous of the likes of Kora or anything concerning me.

"I prefer moonflower wine. It's much more potent and doesn't require eons to finally age. In fact, it's perfect right off the vine."

Swirling his stick over the fire, Roark nods. "Sounds like my kind of brew."

"Oh. Then, well, you must have some. As soon as we make it to Viridia, I'll be sure to make you some. There are plenty of moonflowers in bloom this season," I say, taking a small nibble of the pine nut. I'm trying to eat like a lady, but the minute he rears his head back to eat another helping, I'll plow through this entire stick.

"Pella..." Roark's voice is darker as he continues gazing at the fire.

"Yes, Roark?"

"Earlier, you mentioned regaining your power once you're back on Viridian soil. The things you did earlier—back in the mountain corridor and when you used your mirage—" He pauses, and the way his eyes pierce into mine is like he's looking at me for the first time. I tip my head slightly, interested to see where this is going. "Does it really take a lot of power to use your magic?"

I flutter around in a circle. Talking about myself is always an awkward topic. "Well, yes, but mostly because my power originates from Viridia. I've been gone for such a long time that anytime I use any magic, I run the risk of depleting myself entirely."

Roark's chest rumbles as he sits upright, dropping the stick in the fire.

"What do you mean, deplete yourself? Explain!" he growls, his face showing the ghastly shadow of his Reaper face.

What's gotten into him? His moods certainly vacillate quickly from one emotion to the next. Shrugging my shoulders, I flap my wings hard, hoping to create a little distance.

"Oh no you don't!" he roars, wrapping me in his large palm.

"Take your bloody hands off me!" I yell. "Don't you dare handle me as though I were some child's plaything! You know as well as any that I am not to be touched!"

Roark's eyes narrow as he slowly lessens his grip, still keeping me in his hold. "I'll let you go once you tell me what you mean by deplete."

Sighing hard, I shake my head, wondering why I owe him any explanation. "Well, since it's not immediately obvious to you, Master Reaper, let me make it plain. If I am depleted of my power, I am depleted of my life. It's symbiotic. One cannot survive without the other."

His eyes grow wide with something that looks like fear, and I realize I've done the impossible.

I've struck fear in the heart of a Reaper.

# CHAPTER 28

# Roark

I am at a loss for words. Who knew such a small being could be such an amazing force of strength and honor? Even still...

"Don't you ever do that again!" I grit, making sure she's eye-level with me.

Pella's large, golden-greenish eyes glow bright as she looks up at me. I can't tell if she's frightened, mad, or both. I just hope she understands how serious I am. Before I can ensure she understands, she leans over and bites my finger, forcing me to release my grip.

"Damn it!" I shout. Her small teeth feel like little knives. Once more, I'm impressed.

Flying out of my reach, she spits a heap of dust my way, but when I dodge her, she groans, balling her tiny fists at her side. "And don't you ever do that again! I'll not allow you, a Scullard or anyone else—not even the Great Prince himself—to manhandle me!"

Jumping up, I roar. I've never felt so frustrated. Why doesn't she understand I just want her safe? "You are a piece of work, Pella of Viridia, you know that? A fucking piece of work!"

"Yes, and just like all of male-kind, you think you can control a feminine being on a whim because you're bigger and stronger. Well, I won't be controlled by you or anyone."

"Control? Who is trying to control you? It's not me. I haven't been in control since the moment I came for you. Ditch your guard! Travel this route! Turn into a fucking pixie! And the one time I even dare suggest that you—"

Pella's eyes grow violent like lightning as her wings brighten against her back, creating a vibrant glow. "Do what? What can I do to save myself? Have you ever stopped to wonder why I had to use my mirage in the first place? Or is your first instinct to simply order me around?"

"No, dammit! My first instinct is to keep you safe!"

"What?" Pella snips, tilting her head and squinting as she stares at me with her arms folded.

Taking a deep breath, I do my best to stay calm. "Pella, as much as I appreciate you wanting to get me out of that narrow corridor, you put yourself at risk. I don't want you risking your life to save me."

"But I–I–"

I lift a finger in caution. I've put up with much from her in the short time we've been on this journey; I'm not sure how much more I can tolerate. "Promise me you won't risk your life to save mine."

Shaking her head in protest, Pella frowns. "Roark, I can't promise you that."

Groaning, I let out another sigh. "Why not?"

"Because I can't watch you die."

I stretch my forefinger out toward her; she lands on it and takes slow, graceful steps toward me.

"Death will not consume me as is the manner of some," I whisper, enjoying the way her eyes sparkle when she looks at me.

Pella bats her thick lashes, and I feel something quake inside me. "What do you mean?"

"Only the power of Night itself can bring a finality to my days. So, while the rocks may have indeed crushed me, death cannot prevail against death. It is impossible."

"Oh," she breathes, her shoulders slumping a bit, and she sits down as I turn my palm over. "I guess I risked my power for nothing, huh?"

Using my opposite hand, I let the knuckle of my smallest finger lightly tap her chin. "Nethers no!" I counter, making sure I don't frighten her. "It was an honorable gesture. You are rather stout-hearted for someone so small."

Pella's eyes flit up to mine, and she sticks out her chest. The way her tiny mound of cleavage bounces beneath her leaf covering awakens longings I recently believed frivolous.

"Ready to join the guard, sir!" she shouts, saluting me with a cute grin.

"At ease," I smile, offering her a faux salute of my own. "We still have a good journey ahead of us. We should keep moving."

Swinging her legs, Pella looks up over my head toward the mountains. "It's so pretty," she whispers, her eyes twinkling in admiration. "I remember coming to the Midas Mountains with my family. Seems like ages ago..." she continues, her eyes watering even as she keeps a bright smile on her face.

"You know, I don't know much about you, Pella, save that you are the ward of Prince Kharon. And, of course, that you're from Viridia."

Shrugging her shoulders, her mouth crumples to one side. "Yeah, I don't spend much time talking about myself."

Nodding in agreement, I realize how similar we are. I don't talk much about myself either.

"I can understand," I say. "It's alright. You don't have to talk about your family if you don't want to."

Pella flutters from my arm and circles around a few times. It's clear she's not in the mood to share, so I won't push it. Standing, I wipe the dust from my legs and dump a heap of pine nuts into my satchel. I'm not accustomed to this terrain; there's no telling when we'll get our next meal.

"My mother loved coming here during midsummer," Pella breaks through the silence as she buzzes past me. "The folk of Viridia were excellent miners. Our size and magic allowed us to siphon gold from the far reaches of the mountain. In fact, that corridor is one of the last places we mined before..." Pella stops her fluttering and looks away into the distance.

I turn to the side, allowing her to wipe the diamond-crusted tears now racing down her face.

"Which way?" I ask, pointing to a fork in the road. On one side, there's more of the rocky terrain, and on the other, a small set of withering trees.

"Toward the trees, of course!" Pella's tone is almost as bright as her glowing golden wings. "Follow me!" she exclaims with a wide smile.

Little does she know, I'd follow her anywhere.

"Not only are the folk of Viridia excellent miners, but we're experts in Nether-horticulture. Preservation of the beauty of the land is very important to Viridians," I say, waving my hand around, pointing at the shrubbery and flowers.

Roark only grunts in acknowledgement as his eyes scan the area. He's been practically silent while I've rambled on about Viridia, and his gaze shifts from curious to surprised as we walk along the green landscape. So much of the Netherworld is covered in ash—it's not often we find colors of green, gold, and red here.

Still, it's not as vibrant as I recall from my youth. In fact, it seems quite dreary. I know if my kin were still alive, the forests bordering Viridia would be alive with the beauty of our land. Now, however, it looks like a shell of its former self.

Swallowing the lump welling in my throat, I press on. "Although we're not there yet, you'd usually hear the sounds of singing from afar. Oh, how the folk of Viridia loved to sing!" I exclaim, my hands clasped at my heart.

"Do you sing?" Roark asks, his gaze still wary as we make our way downhill. He's got one hand on the ax in his holster, as though he were waiting for someone to attack any minute.

"No, not anymore," I mutter quickly before flying ahead to a golden berry tree. "Golden berries!" I shriek, surprised to see the fruit ripe and in bloom.

"Golden what?" Roark grouses, coming to my side.

Picking one from the tree, I offer it to him. "Oh, they're quite delicious, Master Reaper. You must try one!"

Laughing, Roark takes the fruit from me. "It's bigger than you!" he chuckles. Frowning, he inspects the fruit in his hand. "I don't see anything gold—just these leaves."

"Do those leaves look familiar?" I smile, waving my hand over my torso.

"Very." He chokes out the word, his gaze dragging over the entirety of me.

"I love using the leaves of fruit trees for my coverall. Keeps me smelling sweet," I giggle, playfully batting my eyes.

Roark's chest rumbles a bit as he stares at me. "Is that so?"

"You should try the fruit," I say, doing my best to get his attention off me.

Plucking the berry from inside the leaf, Roark takes a small bite. "Very good." He nods appreciatively. "So, is this how you taste?" he groans, his eyes flash like lightning.

My throat hitches. "My lord Reaper?" I whisper, wondering if I heard him correctly.

Roark's eyes darken as he watches me, a hungry gaze in his eyes pinning me so that my wings are pressed into the tree behind me. Still, I look away, hoping this isn't what I think it is.

"Please don't eat me!" I call out, pressing my eyes tightly together.

"What?" Roark barks with a lilt of surprise. "Of course not! Why would you think that?"

Opening one eye, I give him a stare. "Sire, you just implied I taste like fruit. How else should I take it?"

Roark's shoulders roll in amusement as he folds his arms over his chest. "I can assure you, I meant it in the best way possible." Sighing, he softens his expression some. "Pella, please know, I didn't mean to frighten you." His tender gaze sweeps over the entirety of me.

"When you said eat me…The Scullards…" I sigh, not sure how much I should share. "They like to feast off my kind," I painfully confess.

Roark's eyes grow wide before narrowing into a more malevolent stare. "Is that what happened to your kin? I know the Great Prince saved you when Viridia was destroyed, but I never knew–"

"I saved myself," I correct him.

Lifting his palm, a warm smile spreads across his face. "My mistake. I should know better. I saw firsthand how you are more than able to take care of yourself."

"It's quite alright," I say, forcing a small smile. "Given my size, most folk assume the Great Prince saved me. He didn't. Well, at least not in the way you think. When I fled to Purgia, he welcomed me with open arms, and for that, I owe him everything."

Grunting once more, Roark's eyebrows draw together. "Everything, huh?" he snorts, dropping the goldenberry to the ground. "We should keep moving."

He doesn't wait for me to respond as he marches off, his boot squashing the fruit under his heavy heel. Once more, I'm sidelined by Roark's whiplashing mood. I'm not entirely sure what crawled up his ass, but I'll choose to shrug it off for now.

With the Great Prince in the earthbound realm, there aren't many left I can count on. The fact that the Reaper lord himself is seeing to my aid is enough for me not to take whatever is going on with him personal.

I make a bee line to his side as we continue through the forest. He doesn't immediately look at me when I buzz around his periphery, but he takes a quick glance, only to turn his sights ahead.

This time, I notice he looks different. A shadow of his typical ghastly features now rests over his face, and I wonder what that means. Normally, he only looks like that when he's preparing for battle. I suspect he's trying to keep himself ready in the event things go awry. Since I'm not sure what's going on in his head, I remain quiet. I don't want to cause him any further alarm.

My wings grow heavy as we continue, and I wish I could rest once more in the hardened ridges of his shoulders. Looking at him, I'm sure there are other hard places where I could rest, but I shake the thought.

*There's no hope for such a thing.*

I'd even take the tight squeeze of his pocket, if only I could give myself a rest. Between using so much of my magic and flying such a far distance, I'm spent. We Vidirdians are sprinters. This cross-country buzzing is not my specialty.

Still, I can't help wondering who soothes the passionate aches of a strong, strapping, chiseled, well-built mammoth of a being like the Reaper lord. Surely no quaint little sprite such as myself could do a creature like him justice.

Well... at least not like this. Perhaps if I– No. I can't. *That is forbidden.*

"It's too quiet."

An odd thing, I know, since I'm accustomed to roaming through Purgia alone. Even though I'm one of the few who can understand the Dark Guard, they aren't much company.

Pella halts her buzzing and turns to face me. "My lord?" she starts, her brow raised in suspicion as she stares around. "Do you sense danger? Is someone coming?"

"No, of course not," I continue. "You've been rather quiet is all." I miss hearing her voice, but I can't tell her that.

"Oh," she giggles, covering mouth bashfully. "I didn't want to bother you, and..."

I shake my head, wagging my finger in protest. "You don't bother me, Pella."

Our eyes lock for a moment, and I see a faint rosy tint blush her cheekbones. She's so fucking adorable. Why does she have to be so incredibly small?

"I don't?" Her voice is small as she flutters to my side, clasping her hands together.

Her small breasts crash together as she does, and I feel vitality rise in my groin. Rotating my holster, I hope she doesn't spy my hardening length bucking to be free.

"Well, that's strange," she continues, buzzing to my side once more.

"How so?" I ask as we make our way through the forest.

"For starters, Thelios always calls me a bother, and the Great Prince, well, he doesn't say it, but I'm sure he thinks the same."

A deep rumble churns through my chest as I stop pacing. "We are not the same," I grit out.

"My lord?"

"The Ferryman. The Grim. The Reaper. We are not the same." I lash my words like a whip, and Pella back peddles away from me.

"Master Reaper," she begins, her tone almost as serious as mine. "Please know I meant no offense, but your moods are quite disarming, to say the least. I mean, one moment, you're fine, and then this." She waves her hand over the entirety of me. "Let me dead level with you, Roark. You've got one more time to bark at me before I–"

Sneering, I lunge toward her—not to hurt her, just to see every inch of her face. I want to know what she looks like when she is upset. I wish to study it, understand her moods, completely and intimately.

"Before. You. What?" I choke out the words. I'm too fixated on just how enchanting she looks with her brows furrowed and her lips puckered. Pella isn't backing herself into any corners this time.

Swallowing hard, she narrows her eyes to match the darkness in mine.

"Before I take my chances with the Scullards. I'll fight them all off if I have to," Pella says, her brow arching with pure hubris. *Fuck,* I love her for it.

Groaning, I circle her. I want to capture her like this from all sides. "You'll never make it a full night's watch."

"Oh, I'll make it alright. On my own moxie, if need be, but I will."

Now I go in for the hard hit. "They'll eat you alive," I say, licking my lips.

Pella's gaze shifts momentarily, and I see her blush once more. "No one is eating me or making me do anything I don't want to do. That, I promise you."

I feel strength rising at my crotch once more, but I do my best to rein in the beast bucking to be free. It's not the mangy beasts I have to protect Pella from; it's the monster between my legs that could surely end her with one hard stroke.

"And you're so sure?" I hissed, holding my hand against my holster, carefully trying to shield my reaction.

Laughing, Pella folds her arms, and her gold wings flutter rapidly at her back. "Oh, Master Reaper, I haven't been surer of anything," she says with a beautiful, sing-song lilt in her voice that sounds like a thousand voices in one.

Before I have a chance to reply, Pella whirls around, creating a shimmering plume that clouds my view of her.

"Pella!" I shout her name into the haze of glimmer. The ground shakes and the trees seem to move, closing in all around me. I've never seen anything like it. "Where are you?" I growl out when I don't immediately hear a response.

A roll of laughter permeates the air, echoing from all sides. "I'm here... I'm here... I'm here..." Pella's words echo among the trees, and the branches shake and flowers bloom as the sound of her voice bounces from limb to limb.

"Where are you?" I shout once more. I feel a cool breeze wash over me as a sweet floral aroma implodes my senses. A light wind brushes along my shoulder, and I turn about, still looking for Pella, but I don't see her.

*Fucking pixie magic,* I inwardly groan, realizing I've been duped.

A bright blast of light shines from the center of the forest as gold ivy pulls from the ground, creating a gate with diamond-like thorns layered throughout. It's as beautiful as it is enchanting, and I find myself holding my breath at the grandeur of it all.

There's one more tap to my shoulder, and this time I turn to find Pella fluttering behind me. "I'm here," she says, her mouth curved to one side as her eyes gleam with pride. She knows I'm in awe of her, and she likes it. "I'm home!" she exclaims, almost breathless.

"Did you do all of this?" I ask, waving my hand around.

Winking at me, she offers a nonchalant shrug. "Come. Let me show you around."

Following after her, we walk toward the golden ivy, and I watch as the thorny limbs stretch out before us, opening like a gate. As we pass through, the golden leaves glow bright as the ivy tethers back together, locking us inside.

Nothing but green and vibrant floral patterns of violet, orange, and yellow flow throughout the misty labyrinth before me. The trees seem to move, and there's a musical tone the leaves and branches make as Pella floats through the verge.

I notice her wings aren't flapping anymore as a small dusting of pixie mist seems to carry her effortlessly along the way. She seems far more relaxed now than she was the last half of the trip, and it makes me wonder if perhaps her wings were tired. I never considered it before, but I suppose how feet get tired of walking, wings do as well.

I make a mental note for our return trip back to Purgia. I'll carry her the entire way if need be. Still, I wish she felt comfortable enough with me to share when she needs help. I must do a better job of taking care of her.

"So this is home?" I say, stopping to observe the shimmering pond in the middle of the garden. There are small lily pads floating throughout, and I imagine this is how small creatures like Pella relax.

"Yes, this is my home!" Pella exclaims, her arms stretching just as wide as her smile as she twirls about. "Do you like it?"

"It's very lovely, Pella. I can see where you get your beauty. Only a beautiful place like this can make such a beautiful creature."

Pella's cheeks glow with a new gold undertone, and she clasps her hands together at her waist as her lashes flit up. "Oh, you're just saying that because I spooked you back at the gate," she continues, brushing her hand against the wind.

"Well, I've never really seen your magic on display at Purgia, but you've shown me you're quite a formidable sprite. After what I've seen of you today, I believe you'll certainly give those filthy beasts a run for it." No sooner do the words leave my mouth that the ground shakes and the vibrant colors among the trees and shrubbery fade to a darkening brown.

"Iremia!" Pella belts, once more with the sound of a thousand voices. Waving her arms around, she extends her fingers toward the trees as a faint glimmering light glows from her palms.

The trees sway, the branches bobbing reverently up and down as she utters the ancient words of calm until the garden returns to its more colorful array.

"What just happened?" I groan, looking around in awe of the transformation of the garden.

"Master Reaper, you should know that Viridia is not just a place. It is a lifeforce all its own. As such, it remembers how it was wronged. When you mentioned the wretched offenders, Viridia became defensive. But not to worry—I assured Viridia you meant no harm."

A lovely purple aura hovers around Pella as she speaks, and I want to freeze this moment in time. Pella didn't merely calm the darkness looming over Viridia; she calmed the darkness in me.

The way Roark is looking at me now is so intense, I don't know whether to fly away or into his arms. I wish I knew what he was thinking.

His expression sits somewhere between intrigue and passion. For whatever life there is in me, I am certain a creature like Roark could never think intriguing or passionate things about me.

Perhaps he still considers how I'd taste? Then again, he assured me he meant no harm. What kind of eating comes without harm, I don't know, and I'm not sure I want to find out.

His mouth curves into a crooked smile as his gaze stays pinned to me. "I meant no offense," Roark offers, his eyes now scanning the tree line. "I am only here to keep Pella safe. I swear on my scythe and all that I am, no harm will come to Viridia or Pella by my hand."

A bright, iridescent light shines around us as metallic leaves fall, revealing the Great Oak, the first tree of the two realms nestled here in my home. Viridian folk have long been the sacred keepers of the Great Oak. Although it typically remains hidden behind the glimmer mist, today, it's choosing to stand tall before the Reaper lord himself.

"Is that?" Roark gulps, his eyes glazed in awe.

"Yes," I answer, flying back and forth in front of Roark, but only the tree is in his sights as a strong gust of wind sweeps through the garden. Golden leaves whirl around us as the branches clank together in a musical pattern. "They're playing a Viridian song of merriment!" I shout to Roark over the ever-growing sounds of music. "The folk of Viridia normally dance and sing."

Roark's brows fold down as his mouth works into a frown. "I don't dance or sing."

Shaking my head, I can't help but laugh at how grumpy he looks, standing there with his large folded arms while the foliage of Viridia does its best to charm him into a jig. The Reaper lord of Purgia will not be moved.

"Pipe down!" I call out, looking around the garden. "At least allow me to show Master Reaper around a bit before we try to coerce him into our ways," I giggle, looking over my shoulder at Roark. "Come." I wave him to my side. "Let me show you my home."

Roark's expression remains tight, but he makes his way to my side. Circling the lake, I reveal my favorite points, from my go-to hiding spots as a rebellious youth to my favorite tree to watch shooting stars. Roark seemed interested enough to hear about all my most memorable moments in Viridia.

"I never knew much about Viridian folk," Roark begins, stopping at a small fountain covered with moonflowers. "Or Viridia in general," he adds as he takes a whiff of the flowers. "But I can see how much your home means to you."

I smile as I fly to sit on the spigot at his eye level. "Thank you. I'm glad you like it. I'm sorry if I got all huffy with you earlier. It's just—"

Roark lifts his palm, shaking his head. "No, I am the one who should apologize. It wasn't right of me to antagonize you."

"And I shouldn't have compared you to the Grim lord or the Great Prince. You are your own creature. I would not want to be compared to a dark fae like Liv, even if we are friends. Not all fae are the same."

"Well she is particularly taller than you," Roark smiles, leaning in and giving me a wink. And damn what a smile it is. With the way his wavy brown hair blows in the wind as he casts a steely stare that has my lady bits beaming with glee, it's a wonder I've never given much thought to just how handsome Roark is.

Turning my head, I shrug my shoulders. "I suppose." I laugh it off; I need to stop staring at him like a lovesick puppy. Even more, I wish I could tell him the truth, but the truth is too dangerous. It's best to change the subject. Standing, I point to the wine flowing from the fountain. "Are you ready to try some moonflower wine, my lord?"

Scratching his jaw, Roark tilts his head just a bit as he narrows his eyes at me. "Trying to get me drunk already, Pella? What will the trees think?" He laughs as he stands. "Actually, I should go have another look around. You know, do a sweep of the perimeter to make sure everything is safe."

"Oh, okay, but you really don't have to do that. We could just send out the blossoms." I smile, pointing to the blossom shrubs.

Quirking his brow, Roark looks at me like I spoke in a foreign tongue. "The blossoms?"

"Why yes, my lord Reaper. For ages, the folk of Viridia have used blossoms to provide security at our borders." Hovering over the shrubbery, I point to the leaves. "They glow red when danger is near. You'll find they are quite adept at alarming us of any ill intent encroaching the area."

"And did you use these blossoms at the last–" He covers his mouth. "*Scullard attack?*" he whispers, hopeful to not create undue alarm as he gives me a stern look.

The thought strikes me right in the gut. I know he's not being cheeky, but it's a fair question.

My fingers find themselves clasped together in my usual nervous response. "Well, I suppose they're more of a warning signal than protection."

Roark's dark gaze softens as he looks at me, and his mouth draws into a thin line, like he wants to say more but is restraining himself. "I see." He lets out a small sigh. "How about you show me how the blossoms work after I check out the perimeter? That way, I can advise you of any failings. Makes sense to have more blossoms near your weakest points."

Affirming with a brief nod, I work up a smile. If Roark wanted to be an arrogant, know-it-all general right now, he could be. I've seen him in action. I know what he's capable of. Instead, he's doing his best to take a gentler approach with me.

"Besides, this is your home. The final say rests with you. I'll only advise, if that's okay with you."

My heart warms within me. I've never seen this side of Roark. I always think of him as this ax and scythe wielding barbarian of sorts. Now he's more of a gentle giant. And I love it.

"That sounds like a good idea. Whatever advice you can offer, I'll accept, my lord."

Once more, his brow raises as he tilts his head to me. "Please, just Roark."

"After you, Roark," I smile, offering a slight curtsy.

Extending his arm toward me, he gives a small bow. "After you."

Buzzing to his side, I land on his shoulder. "How about together?"

He shoots me a wink. "Together sounds perfect to me."

# CHAPTER 32

# Roark

"Here's your problem right here," I say, kneeling to point to a grouping of withered ivy along the border. "There's definitely a breach here at the south end gate. Did you know the branches had desiccated?"

Pella shakes her head, her eyes glazing with tears. "These are the oldest branches of the great tree," she explains, pointing back to the large golden oak in the middle of the garden. "The old ones always said as darkness spreads in both realms, the power of the Great Oak would fade."

While I never put much stock in the legends and mysticism of the Great Oak, even I understand just how troubling this is.

"This must be how they got in before. There's a large enough hole here to usher in a whole horde," I groan, staring at the flimsy branches and the once-golden leaves that are now brown and crumpled on the ground. "I can try to tighten it up, but it could take some time."

"How can I help?"

I'm appreciative of her offer, but there's really nothing she can do. I can use my scythe to pull the limbs back together, but I'll still need to manually weave each limb through the gate.

"You can send blossoms here to the south end and then scatter the rest around the remaining perimeter. That should give us a decent warning should any threats arise."

"Are you sure you don't want me to help you with the vines?"

Pella's donning a bright smile, but I know better. She needs her rest. After she flew off my shoulders when I started inspecting the vines, she was once again aided by the glimmer mist. Even now, she looks like she can barely keep herself afloat. If it weren't for the cloudy mist helping her, she'd probably faint.

"Absolutely not!" I quip as Pella's eyes narrow, and I know I'm tapping on her nerve. I need to fix this. "Listen, Pella, this is a really easy job for me. You, on the other hand, need some rest."

"What makes you think I'm so tired?"

"I'll answer if you can promise me you'll let me know if you're too tired to fly on our return trip to Purgia."

She gasps, and Pella's thick lashes flutter up to the sky before drifting back to me. "I–I don't know what—"

Pulling my scythe out from my back holster, I lay it at my side. "Oh, I think you know perfectly well what I mean. Why didn't you tell me you were exhausted earlier? I would have carried you, and properly, I might add. I wouldn't place you in my pocket if it didn't suit your fancy."

"How–how did you know?"

I lean in so my face is level with her. "You'll soon learn just how much you capture my attention."

Clasping her hands together, Pella's lips curve to one side as she swallows hard. "I'm just not used to asking for help, is all."

"No. Not unless it's Kharon," I groan, chucking my scythe deep in the ground to pull up some roots. I can hardly believe I said that out loud.

Buzzing around me so that she's in my face, Pella lands on the curved point of my blade just before I strike the ground once more. My eyes blaze with fire, fueled by her recklessness.

"Don't worry about me," Pella answers quickly, her small hands trailing the length of my blade. She has no idea how good that feels. My blade and I are one; I can feel the gentle touch of her fingers gliding over the cool steel as if it were my own skin.

Tremors erupt through me as I do my best to hold back how I feel. I hardly think she knows just how connected I am to scythe. Maybe if she did, she wouldn't be touching it as she is now.

"I promise I saw the blade. You're not the only one who pays close attention." Smiling, Pella crosses her legs, and the sight of her curved thigh resting on my scythe makes my mouth water. "Besides, that's the second time you've gotten defensive when I've mentioned the prince. Is there something going on that I should know about?"

A low growl rumbles through me. "Is there something *I should know*?" I grunt, yanking a heap of ivy from the ground. The thorns cut through my fingers, drawing blood, but I don't give a damn.

"About Kharon?" Pella grouses, shrugging her shoulders.

Throwing the ivy aside, I wipe my hands across my shoulder. Pella's eyes grow wide when she sees the blood, and she parts her lips to say something, but I hardly care about these wounds. They'll heal just fine. But if she tells me there's more going on with her and Kharon, I don't think *that* wound will ever heal.

"No! About *you and Kharon*!" I bark, showing her my palm so she can watch my scars heal before her eyes.

Pella remains quiet as she waits for the last mound of flesh to tether in place. Swallowing hard, she looks away from me and back again. "There is no me and Kharon. I am simply his ward. You know this." Her gaze locks with mine like she's mining for secrets, but I have none to tell. "But what I want to know is why you're so worked up."

Shifting so my back is against a small tree, I sigh, resting my arm over my knee. "Is it so difficult to guess?" I mumble, not sure whether she heard me. Before she has an opportunity to put it together, I keep going. "You just seem rather loyal to the prince–you know, for a ward."

Shaking her head, Pella's shoulders roll in amusement. "I could say the same for you, Master Reaper. You are his right hand, are you not?"

Groaning, my head falls back onto the tree trunk. "That's not the same."

"How so? And please don't say because you're male-kind and I'm not," she exclaims.

"Well... "

Gasping, Pella gives me a hearty eye roll. "You can't be serious! I always thought you a brute, a barbarian even, but misogynistic? I never thought—"

"I'm hardly a pig, Pella!" I counter, swiping my hand through the air. "But you do oversee his harem, and traditionally those who do–"

A bright white light blares like lightning around me as Pella springs up from her place on the edge of my blade. Once my eyes refocus, I see her hovering in front of me, her hands on her hips and her pretty little mouth crouched to one side.

"Then I suppose I'm the first virgin to lead a harem! Perhaps, Master Reaper, you can find a more suitable place to shove your antiquated definition of tradition!"

Just when I thought I couldn't care for her any more than I already did, I am irrevocably and completely under her spell—not simply because she's shared something so intimate with me, but because she stood up to me.

I am the Reaper. I tear souls, ripping them to shreds like wheat in my own dark harvest. I have no need for charity or the pity of grace, but there's something in her shimmering gaze, enchanting me to places my vagrant soul cannot comprehend.

Her cheeks blush as her eyes shimmer an almost blinding hue. I know Pella is embarrassed to have revealed so much in her anger, but I need her to know she can share anything with me.

"I'm sorry," I begin, stretching out my hand. "I know it's not my first apology, and it likely won't be my last, but I didn't mean to offend you again." Pausing, I watch as she takes small steps into my palm, her wary gaze ensuring I don't curl my hand. "It's just, the thought of you with anyone else–"

"Anyone else?" she repeats, her brow lifting with intrigue. "Look at me," she grouses, waving her arms over her torso.

My eyes travel from head to toe. *She is perfect!* "I am looking at you." I nearly choke out the words.

"Then you can see how that would be a problem. Overseer of the harem of the high court or not, there's absolutely no one else! I'm just this, this little thing who flies around."

Pulling my hand close to my chest, I lightly graze my small end finger along her arm. Touching her feels like silk. If this is what mortals call goosebumps, then I have them.

"You're hardly a little thing, Pella." I smile, watching as her eyes look up to mine. "Maybe others haven't paid much attention, but I am now. I hope that counts for something. I am glad for one thing, though."

Dropping to her knees, she folds her legs under her bottom and looks up. "What?"

"You just told me I have no competition."

# CHAPTER 33

# *Pella*

My mouth drops open—I know I didn't hear him correctly.

"Competition?" I whisper, shyly looking away from Roark's searing-eye stare.

The way he's looking at me...

He moves his hand so I'm once more locked in his gaze, and I'm surprised to find longing in his eyes. Never would I dream that the Reaper of the Netherworld could look at me as his heart's desire, but here he is.

"Does that frighten you?" Roark's tone is quiet, but his voice sends shivers through my soul.

"Yes," I squeak out, searching his face. I wish I knew what was going on in his mind.

"Pella, you have nothing to fear from me. I promise you." Roark looks at me with such gentle care, like a bird with a broken wing. Perhaps he pities me? "I'm just glad to know no one else can get in the way of how I feel for you."

"How you feel for me?" I whisper, looking down and shaking my head in disbelief.

Roark's large thumb rolls over my face, lifting it up so our eyes meet. Cracking a weak smile, he laughs, and I can't help admiring the sexy sweep of his mustache as it curls around his lips. I imagine getting lost in the warm comfort of his beard, what it would be like to roll around naked in that long mane, letting the soft fiber caress every inch of me.

"Yes, Pella. How I feel for you," he repeats. "In case it's not entirely clear, what you heard earlier was jealousy. I thought you and the prince—"

Jumping up, I grab my stomach, nearly nauseous at the thought. "Oh Nethers, no!" I shriek. "That's disgusting!" I grimace, shaking at the mere mention.

Surprise fills Roark's face. "Woah," he laughs. "I see I was wrong."

"Wrong?" I throw my head back and sigh hard. "You were so far from the truth!" I exclaim with my arms outstretched.

"Then why don't you tell me the truth, Pella," he commands, his tone drier than before.

"I don't know what you mean. I've already told you that we're in no way romantic, and there's no one else so—"

"Oh, there is someone else. Me," he grits out, his sharpened stare digging a hole in my heart that he alone wants to fill. "But we'll get to that later," he grumbles. "Now, however, I want the truth. If there's nothing romantic between you, then why has Kharon decreed you forbidden? No one is to touch you, and he keeps you locked up in the High Court. Why? If there's nothing more between you, why would he issue such a decree? Tell me!"

Flying out of Roark's grip, I circle the shrubbery. I need to collect my thoughts. Between hearing Roark declare his feelings for me and what he is demanding now, I can barely think straight.

Before I have an opportunity to fly off, Roark captures me once more. "Not so fast!" he growls.

"My lord, please!" I shout. "It is forbidden!"

"To touch you?" he snarls, pulling me close to his face, breathing me in. "What about to smell you?" He moans against my torso, and my body quakes having him so close to me. "What about to taste you?" Roark whispers, slowly pulling me away as he licks his lips.

My heart freezes. "You said you wouldn't eat me!" I protest, pushing away from his needful stare.

Roark's eyes darken, narrowing like crescent moons as he watches me. "Only not in the way you think."

Frowning, I shrug my shoulders. "What does that mean?"

"No worries, love. I'll tell you what it means when the time is right. For now, I want to know why the prince has made you off limits."

Sighing, I roll my eyes. "Why do you need to know this? Shouldn't we be securing the perimeter?"

Opening his hand, he releases me as he roars, throwing his hands to his head. "You are one exhausting little creature!"

"The pleasure is all mine." I give him a fake curtsy.

Groaning, Roark's pained look of exhaustion is wearing thin as he lets out a small laugh. "So this is the way it's going to be between us, eh?"

"What do you mean?" I ask.

"I demand things. You evade me. You win. I lose."

Fluttering closer, I examine his face; he looks beat. "I don't want you to lose, my lord, but I'm not sure there's any prize to be had by knowing the truth. Besides, some secrets aren't mine to share."

Roark doesn't say anything; he just watches me as his fingers twirl between the ivy at his side.

Swallowing hard, I move closer. "I can tell you, at least from my side, why I am forbidden, but you must promise never to tell a soul, not even the Grim lord."

Lifting two fingers, now smeared with his blood from the thorns of the ivy, he draws his mouth into a thin line. "With my own blood, I swear it."

"You'll have to stand for this one, Master Reaper," I say, motioning for him to rise. "Please know that I am only telling you this because, as my protector, you at least deserve to know what you are protecting." I pause for a moment, hopeful we agree. He gives me a brief nod, letting me know I can continue. Waving my hand along the ground where the flowerbed and ivy meet, I point to a small stream. "Do you see where this stream leads, my lord?"

Roark walks along the stream. Nearing the forest edge, he stops and places his hand over his eyes to see into the distance.

"Yes. From here, it looks like it flows into the Styx and the Acheron. I never knew that!" Roark says, throwing a small smile over his shoulder. "But what does that have to do with anything?"

I let out a sigh. Here goes nothing.

"Remember when I told you Viridia and I are one in the same? Symbiotic?" I wait, hopeful he understands. His eyes narrow a bit, and I think he's catching on. "Well, the same power of Viridia that flows in my veins also flows into both the Styx and the Acheron. Now, you've been in Purgia and around the Great Prince long enough to know his origins, am I correct?"

Roark's eyes grow wide, his mouth opening and closing repeatedly as reality sets in. "Wait a minute; are you saying... "

"Yes, my lord. The power of the Great Prince comes from the waters that flow from Viridia. I am all that is left of not only my people, but Viridia itself. If anything were to happen to me... "

Folding his arm over his chest and resting his fist at his chin, Roark paces back and forth. "I can't believe I never knew this," he gasps, his gaze shifting between me and the stream. "I'm surprised Kharon never told me. Then again, I can understand his hesitation."

"Precisely. If others knew what I truly meant to him–"

"They'll never learn it from me!" Roark quickly interjects. "I vowed to protect the Great Prince long ago. I pledge that no harm will ever come to you, not by my hand or any other."

My eyes water a bit. It feels like a weight has been lifted.

"Thank you, Roark," I smile, wiping a loose tear from my cheek.

"But wait a minute!" Roark grumbles. "Is that why they captured you? Do they know?"

A grim smile crowds the side of my face. "No, those wretched beasts know nothing. They're just quite carnivorous during their breeding season."

Scratching his beard, Roark's eyes narrow once more. "Yeah, that's the strange part. It is their breeding season. They should be out looking for able bodies to infect with their wretchedness, not pursuing one lone fae."

The true reason behind those wretched beasts pursuing me is not a secret I wish to share so soon. I think I've shared enough.

"Then again—you know what, it doesn't matter," Roark groans, shaking himself out of whatever just crossed his mind. "You're right—we should secure the perimeter. But first, I want to thank you."

I give a weak smile. I'm just thankful to move on from the Scullards. "For what?"

"For sharing a little bit of yourself with me. I'm looking forward to you sharing even more."

My breath hitches as his eyes lock with mine, and it finally becomes clear: the Reaper wants me to share more than secrets, and he has no idea just how eager I am to bare it all to him.

That should do it. Tugging my scythe through the soil, I pull the last vine through, threading it together. It should hold the gate together, preventing anyone from getting in too easily. I wish I could make it tighter, but it's the best I can do for now.

Standing, I look around and take in the sight before me. Viridia is a beautiful place, far more majestic and filled with light than any other place in the Netherworld. While Purgia is certainly regaled with grandeur, perfect for Netherfolk seeking to spend their life's end, Viridia is a fitting origin of splendor and beauty. It's no wonder a creature as lovely as Pella was birthed from the very soil of this sacred land.

Yet, as beautiful it is, without Pella, it is nothing.

Little did I know when I set out to save her, I was not only ensuring the life of the Great Prince, but the very core of all Netherfolk and even some in the earth realm–any who are tethered by the power of this Great Oak.

Although I grow fonder of Viridia with each passing moment, not having Pella at my side gnaws at my very soul.

This is probably the longest we've been apart since I took her away from the Scullards. If it weren't for the intermittent flashes of light letting me know she's added another heap of blossoms in the field, I wouldn't know where she was.

Strangely, it's the quiet that's getting to me. When Pella is around, there's endless chatter, or if nothing more, the buzzing sound of her wings flapping at my side. Now, there's nothing.

In all my time as Reaper, I've never given much thought to what it would be like to have a partner by my side, someone to walk this Netherworld with, to argue, to laugh, *to love*—to do it all. Companionship; that's what Pella has given me.

I want more, but I'll be content for as long as I can at least have her in my life. Always.

Throwing my scythe into the saddle on my back and adjusting my ax in my holster, I realize it's been a minute since I've seen any flashes of light from Pella. It's way too quiet for my liking.

Making my way back to the center of the garden, my eyes scan the area for Pella. A knot swells in my throat at the sickening thought that perhaps the creatures snuck in and took her right from under me. Marching back and forth, I circle the tree line a few times, hopeful I'll catch her still arranging blossoms in the field. Still, she's nowhere to be found.

"Pella!" I roar so loud, the branches shake. "Pella!" I growl out once more, turning toward the front entrance to check the gate. Everything looks in place, but I can't see her.

"Hey!" I hear her sing-song voice call from below. "I'm down here!" she giggles, and the sound of water splashing draws my attention.

Exhaling a hard breath, I'm overcome with relief when I find Pella laying on a lily pad, drifting around the pond.

A small, albeit exasperated, chuckle escapes me as I kneel to see her floating around the moonflower fountain in the center.

"Taking a load off?" I tease, spinning my hand around in the water.

"Hey!" she fusses, holding onto the sides of the lily pad. "Don't spin me around!" Pella laughs, making waves with her feet against the water. She *wants* me to spin her.

"Having fun, eh?" I laugh.

Throwing her hands over her head, Pella smiles wide, like she doesn't have a care in the world. She is a marvel! How someone so small, yet who carries such a lofty weight, can relax as if all is well in her world is beyond me.

My eyes intermittently examine the gates and tree line, hopeful her merriment isn't too short-lived. Seeing her happy like this does something to my soul. Typically, Pella is doing as she's told, carrying out the Prince's orders and managing some of the light affairs of the High Court. I don't think I've ever seen this carefree side of her, and fuck, I want to see more.

"Come on in!" Pella squeals, splashing her foot against the water toward me. "The water's fine!"

Groaning, I give her a stare. "I don't think this pixie pond was made for my size, love."

Leaning over the lily pad, Pella pokes out her bottom lip as she lays her head on her arm.

Then, the strangest thought comes to mind.

"Pella," I start, running my hand through the water. "Did you finish putting the blossoms in place?"

Rolling back onto the lily, Pella rolls her eyes closed, still poking out her lip. "Yes, yes, all my chores are done, my lord." Sucking her teeth, she frowns and mumbles something I can't hear.

I ignore her grumbling. "And do you feel strong? I mean, now that you're back here in Viridia."

Opening one eye with a quirked brow, she shoots me a hard stare. "Strong enough. Why?"

Standing up, I circle the pond once more, giving a quick cursory glance to make sure everything looks secure.

"Roark!" Pella calls after me, fluttering up to my side. "What's wrong? Are the blossoms in bloom?"

"No, it's nothing like that." My tone is calmer than even I expected, considering what I'm about to say.

Frowning, Pella searches my face. "Then what's wrong? Look, I know I was lounging, but I thought I could—"

"I want you to use the pixie orb on me again." I blurt it out so fast, I don't give myself a chance to reconsider.

Pella's eyes widen as her mouth gapes open. Blinking and shaking her head rapidly, Pella's expression goes from flattered to confused.

"You want me to do what?" she says, slower than I've ever heard her speak.

"The orb, like you did in the mountains. Do that again." No need to reconsider. I want this.

Gasping, she scrambles away from me. "Roark, you can't be serious! Why?"

"I want to hold you, that's why. Since the moment I got you out of that camp, all I've wanted to do is hold you. Not in my palm, but in my arms. That's where you belong, Pella of Viridia, and I want you there now."

For the first time in my existence, I am at a loss for words.

"Pella, did you hear me? I want you in—"

"I heard you." My words rush out, but I'm still in shock.

"So?" Roark says, taking a step closer. "Will you put me back in your orb so I can hold you?"

Swallowing hard, I shake my head, trying to brush off his words. "I can't."

"Why?"

"It's forbidden! You know this!"

A low growl rumbles through Roark's chest as he takes another step. "What if I don't care?"

"And what if I do?"

Stretching his legs wide, he nearly leaps in front of me. I want to move, to just fly away, but I can't. My wings feel stuck, just the sight of him bolting me in place. From the way his dark eyes dance with a melancholy that delights my soul to the gentle sway of his long hair blowing in the breeze, and even the arrogant smirk that has my lady parts twirling with glee, the Reaper of Purgia has me right where he wants me: breathless and panting.

"Then tell me," he whispers against my face, his cool breath making my wings flutter. I inhale the sweet, smoky scent clinging to his beard, and I want to drown myself in its depths.

"Tell you what?" I whisper back, his watchful eye taking in the whole of me.

"Tell me you don't want me to hold you. Tell me you don't want to feel my arms wrapped around your body. Say that you don't want to know how good your body feels pressed against mine."

My voice is raspy, dry, with nothing left to give.

"Say it," Roark demands, and something else flutters in my core I've never felt before.

"Roark, it would be nothing short of a mirage, a phantom at best. What good would it be to taste something so forbidden only to never pick from the vine again?"

Cupping my jaw with the light strum of his small end finger, he offers a soft grin. "Beloved, if you are to be my forbidden fruit, then I'd gladly die on the vine for just a bite."

Palming my face, I shake my head in disbelief. "But why me? Not like this. If only I could—"

Gingerly prying my hands from my face, Roark keeps his forefinger steady, allowing me to rest on him. "I know there are so many reasons we should resist. The prince. Protecting Viridia. Protecting you. But I don't think I can go another minute without you, Pella. I've lived in the shadow of my own loneliness for so long, I never knew I was alone. Then came you. You challenge me, correct me, you even protect me. I never want to be without you. I—"

With that, I don't need to hear another word. Twirling my wrist, I blow a heap of pixie dust into his face, and Roark shrinks in less than a blink of an eye.

"Love you," Roark finishes, his eyes wide with amazement as the golden orb surrounds us both.

He doesn't take much time to look at himself or the orb before he's lifting me up into his arms and crushing his mouth to mine.

*My first kiss.*

Not the ones my late parents gave or the one I doted on my now-departed younger brother. This kiss is different.

His lips are smoother than I'd imagined they would be, cool even, but it's his tongue taming mine into submission, teaching me where to go and how to move as he glides and tethers his tongue with mine.

Roark's lips are gentle but demanding, like he's afraid this moment will pass us by. Thankfully, I'm stronger now than I was in the mountains. We can go on like this for as long as he likes.

My fingers find their way to his beard, my hand brushing through the strong, pillowy texture of his hair, holding on for dear life.

But it's the sweet way Roark is holding me that has every part of me leaping for joy. His large hands are tucked just under my rear as one of my legs hook around his waist. I'm sure he was afraid to wrap his arms around my wings, so he naturally opted to go lower. While I'm glad he did, it won't be long before he discovers my other secret.

"Pella," Roark moans against my mouth. "Please tell me I'm dreaming. That this can't be real." Our heads now touch crown-to-crown as the orb guides us back down to the lily pad.

"Maybe you died," I giggle, pounding my fist against his brawn chest. "Perhaps I am the death dealer now," I purr, playfully baring my teeth.

Locking his arms around me, he growls into the nape of my neck before turning my face to meet his. "If this is death, I'd die a thousand times to be in its embrace."

"Ah..." I moan, feeling Roark's hands now gliding over my backside. "You are not dead, my lord, and this is not a dream. This is very... very real," I choke out the words.

"So you mean to tell me, now that I finally have you in my arms and have laid my lips on yours—now I've discovered you're not wearing knickers. No bottoms. Nothing."

Giggling, I cover my mouth. "Nope."

"All this time?"

Shrugging my shoulders, I bite my nail while leaning against his massive chest. "Sprites like me really don't have a need. The leaves normally keep me covered fairly well."

"Well this is problematic," Roark groans, and I frown, wondering where this is going. "For starters, when we return to Purgia, we'll have to find you something more suitable, because if anyone ever sees what belongs to me—"

Pushing back some, I give him a stare. "What belongs to you?" Twitching my nose, I roll my eyes. "That's rather presumptuous after one kiss, don't you think?"

Roark's eyes darken to black. "In a moment, I'll show you just how much it belongs to me."

My tummy tightens. There's something about his demanding tone that makes me want to obey. He could ask me to crawl right now, and I'd willfully drop to my knees. I'm still trying to hold onto a shred of my strength, but I'm losing it with each passing second.

"Now, let me look at you," he says, slowly letting me slide down his massive body. Even in pixie form, he's a stunning boulder of a creature. I hit the hard, rock-like formation between his legs, and I can't control the needful grunt that escapes at the feel of him against my sex.

Smirking, Roark knows just what he's doing to me, but he's taking his time, savoring each moment. Licking his lips, his eyes roam over my body like he wants to devour me whole.

# CHAPTER 36

# *Roark*

I'm doing my damndest to rein in every dark and depraved desire I have to make her body my personal fucktoy.

The Great Prince would end me if he knew the thoughts I have for his ward. She is forbidden. No one can touch her, but I want to do more than touch her, so I will. I will reap what is mine.

Pella's perky, perfect breasts crowd between the woven leaves adorning her, and it's taking every bit of restraint not to rip the leaves from her body, but I don't want to hurt her.

"You are beautiful, love," I say, gently strumming my hand along her arms. Taking her hand in mine, I pull her close, resting her firmly against my chest. The way her small arms wrap around my waist, like she never wants to let go, makes my soul leap.

Lowering us to the base of the lily pad, I take another moment to just look at her.

"What?" Pella says, a bashful smile curving the side of her mouth. "Aren't you going to take a moment to enjoy the sights from my vantage point? I don't know how much longer the orb will last." As she points around the purple evening sky, Pella's bright eyes flit to the stars.

Pella makes a good point, but I don't give a damn about looking at the stars right now. I can see enough in my periphery to know I'm no bigger than a measure of wheat and Pella a blade of grass, but none of that matters in this moment. Right now, all I can think about is keeping her in my arms.

Combing my hands through the lush, violet strands that now lay against her face, I marvel at the brilliance of the glittering gold illuminating her skin and the sweet gape of her luscious mouth as it lays open, full of wanting.

"Well, that's the second thing I started to say earlier. Since I do have a unique vantage point, it's time for me to not only capture the sights from the sky but delight myself in the most forbidden fruit. That is, if you'll let me."

Pella's head bobs to one side, her gaze narrowing with an innocence that makes me feel dirty for what I'm about to do to her.

"Let you what?"

Trailing my hand down her chin, over her breasts and down to her waist, I hover my hand over her sweet spot. "I want to touch you here." I tap the top of her pussy, and I'm delighted to feel her soft, cottony curls as my finger glides over her slick folds.

Shit. She's already wet.

"You–you're already touching me," she moans, her hips circling, drawing me inside her.

"Do you want me to stop?"

Moaning, Pella cries out beneath me. "No. Don't stop."

"You like that, love? You like the feel of me touching you here?"

Bobbing her head fast, Pella whines. "Yes. Please!" Grabbing my hand, she glides my finger deeper.

"Fuck, baby!" I growl out. "You feel like silk."

Twirling and twisting my finger, I find that sensitive nub and grind my thumb against it until she quivers in my grip.

If I were in the harem, I would have inspected her body from head to toe, but this is different. I'm so damn eager to just be inside her, I can't think straight. I wish to the Night I could drive my length inside her right now, but I fear it would knock us out of the orb, and I'd literally split Pella in two.

Pella's grinding her needy little pussy on my finger like she's been waiting for this moment longer than I can imagine, but I'm not ready for her to come just yet. Pulling out of her, I go to lick my finger when I notice it is covered in liquid gold.

"What the–" I rasp, taking a long lick of my forefinger.

"I–I'm sorry. Did I do something wrong?" Pella's innocent eyes cut up to mine, and I need to do all I can to replace the apprehension I see there.

"No, my sweet girl," I say, stroking the side of her face with my thumb. "Looks like I've struck gold." I part her legs, finally beholding perfection before me. "Damn, baby! That's one fine little pussy. A sweet golden fleece made just for me, glistening and dripping with gold. I've never seen something so pretty."

Once more, Pella's thick lashes flutter as she reaches out, trailing her small hands along my abs down to my waist.

"What's that look you're giving me then?" she asks, her speculative gaze watchful as I crawl between her legs.

"Well, I lied to you when I said I wouldn't eat you, because that's exactly what I'm about to do."

Her eyes are laced with confusion, but I don't give her a moment to protest. When she cries out my name as I thrust my tongue into her opening, I know I have all the permission I need.

Pella's nectar runs like a river over my tongue, nourishing the cold darkness inside me with light and warmth. I'm kissing her outer lips, sucking her juices, brutally fucking her with my tongue until I'm deafened by the crowd of her petite thighs on either side of my head.

"Roark!" she screams, and the colors of the forest glow brighter than before. "R-Roark! I–I–"

With no other warning, the buzzing feel of her clit knocking against my tongue as she drenches my beard with her glittering gold orgasm sends tremors of pure joy through me.

"Mine!" I growl into her sex, issuing one more brutal thrust that has her convulsing with a tight grip on my hair.

"Yours," she coos as her legs fall limp.

She's spent, just how I wanted her. One day, we'll manage to get her full of me.

Rolling her to the side, I nestle her into me so that her rear is flush against my dick. I take Pella's hand in mine as we look up. A shooting star blazes through the sky, and Pella weakly lifts her finger. "Make a wish," she dreamily whispers with a small giggle.

That's exactly what I do.

I wish to the Fates, to the Great Oak, to Night itself to find favor upon me—that this moment not be fleeting, but forever. *I want forever with this woman.* Not simply to comfort my loneliness or because she just flooded my beard with gold. No, I want forever because she has a heart of gold, a heart that would rather ensure the whole of the Netherworld is safe rather than seek her own joy.

Pella is pure gold, and she deserves this kind of bliss on her face every damn day.

# Pella

No sooner did the star glaze the sky did the orb fade. It was harder than I planned to hold my magic steady while Roark feasted on me like a starved man.

At least now, I know what he means when he says he wants to eat me.

I'm not sure how I've missed that term among those in the harem, but since Kharon barely has use for any of them since my arrival, there's not much sexual chatter. Well, there's always gossip about Thelios, but I don't stick around for those details.

Roark, on the other hand, I never hear much about. Most seem too fearful to be around a man of his massive size. While I can understand their hesitation, they have no idea what they're missing.

Although I've returned to my pixie size, I'm happy to just lay in the tangles of Roark's cuddly beard while he rests. I gave him a lily pad full of moonflower wine, and he served himself another round. He didn't wait for me to caution him on the potency, so when his eyes grew heavy, I took the time to lounge, in the pure afterglow, within his mane.

Netherfolk don't sleep often, but when it happens, it falls fast, so I need to use this opportunity to replenish my powers.

Poking around his face a few times, I'm comforted by the rumbling his chest makes as he turns to his side, overcome by the wine. A small smile crosses my face when I see the apt look of peace wash over his face. Knowing I'm responsible for it delights my heart.

~

Diving into the waters, I'm thankful to be home. With every stroke, I soak up the strength of Viridia in my veins. My ancestors call out to me, linking their magic with mine as each majestic drop of water covers my body.

Then, I hear it: singing, the sound of a thousand voices calling out to me in a ballad so sweet, so pure, my soul sings in harmony.

The leaves join in a chorus of the whole of Viridia as the branches match their rhythm with our joyous song. *The Daughter of Viridia Has Returned.*

That's who I am.

I almost forgot.

My heart rejoices as I wind through the water, belting out one final note as an iridescent spray showers me with the wellspring of Viridia itself. My wings flutter rapidly, lifting me out of the water as an aura of golden light from the Great Oak shines upon me, sending strength to my core, linking the full power of my people within me.

Stretching out, I look from my fingers down to my toes, and the sheer energy now flowing through my veins burns within me.

The light of the oak slowly fades as I drift back to the pond, and my feet barely touch the water when the sound of a loud gasp comes from the fern hole banking near the pond.

"Pella!" Roark cries out, his large palm covering his mouth in shock.

177

A small smile covers my face as my wings flap against my back, hovering me just over the water.

"You–you're bigger!" he calls out, wagging his finger at me.

My eyes grow wide in horror. I hadn't realized I'd shifted from my pixie size. I shriek as my wings fold over my naked body, shielding me from his watchful glare.

Turning away from him, I fly to the opposite side of the fern hole. "Roark, I–I can explain. I–ooh–um–"

But Roark is quick, and he's there to meet me before my feet touch the ground. "Pella," he says, grabbing the top of my shoulders. "How is this possible? I woke up and saw you floating up to the Great Oak, and then there was this light and singing and—"

Dropping my chin low, I can't bear to look him in the eyes. "I'm sorry, Roark. I've deceived you."

Stepping back, Roark groans. "Pella, love, what's going on? Whatever it is, you can tell me." Taking my chin in his hand, he lifts my face up to meet his steely, caring eyes.

"I'm sorry. I wanted to tell you sooner, but I didn't know how. I mean, earlier, when you asked to go into the orb, I wanted to say more, but then I–"

"Pella, please, calm down. There's nothing you can say that will scare me away from you." Roark's hand holds my face firm, ensuring I keep my eyes on him. "Just tell me what happened."

"That's just it: nothing happened. This is me. This is my normal size."

Roark's hand drops from my face, and my skin goes cold. I never knew I'd miss his touch so much, but I do.

Running his hands through his hair, he rocks on his heels. "But that's not possible. You're a pixie! Pixies are small and—"

"According to who?" I quietly refute.

Astonished, Roark's eyes travel back to mine as he continues shaking his head in disbelief. "But all this time, you've been small, and we just— the orb–how?"

Heaving a hard sigh, I swallow my angst, knowing I owe him the truth. I love him too much to lie any further.

"It's a long story, but the easiest way to say it is just that it's part of our lore. For ages, descendants of fae like us sprites, or as most call us, pixies, have been hunted to near extinction. Whether it be the sinister pursuit of the Changeling witches, Hades, Scullards or even mortals, we've had to do what we could to evade our own demise. Some, like Liv and the fae of Kilgo Falls, turned to dark magic to ensure their protection. Those of us who remain with the light magic hide our true nature to protect our secrets."

A dark scowl crests over Roark's face, and I fear I'm losing him. But if my truth drives him away, then so be it. If I am to ever be loved for who I am, I have to lay it all on the line.

"And what are your secrets?" he sneers, resting his knuckles against his chin as he watches me.

Taking another deep breath, I continue. "As you know, light magic rests within me. As a carrier of light magic, lifeblood flows through my veins. There are only a handful of Netherfolk with light magic, and those with lifeblood can procreate."

"Wait–so you mean–" Growling, Roark's face flashes into his ghastly reaper form, and a tinge of fear trickles up my spine. "Is that why the Scullards were after you?" His eyes grow wide, full of anger and malice. "You mean to tell me those wretched things were looking to breed you with their blasphemous offspring? That's why they were trying to make you grow?"

A river of tears raced to my chin as I look away from him. I know he must be disappointed in me. "Yes," I cry, a sickening knot churning in my gut.

I don't have a chance to wipe my face when I feel Roark pull me into his arms. "They'll never touch you!" he grunts, lifting my face to see his hallowing glare. I almost want to scream as I lock eyes with the reaper lord of the Netherworld. There's nothing but darkness there, no shadow of turning—just a void made of death and destruction.

For some reason, I don't fear what I see looking back at me, for what is looking back at me is a promise. A covenant. A vow. Nothing will ever hurt me, and he will end every and anything that seeks to harm me. Death and destruction will follow anyone who tries to take me from him, and more than anything, his eyes tell me that vengeance will come swiftly to all who deserve it.

"Do you understand?" Roark growls as his gangly flesh stretches across his skeletal chin.

Reaching up, I strum the side of his boney jaw. "Yes, my lord." I reverently bow my head before burying my face in his hollow chest.

There's no heart there—just withered flesh and bone—but if I didn't know better, I'd swear I heard something resembling a heartbeat. Whatever it is, I don't care. I'm just thankful to be in his arms, where I belong.

"Thank you, Roark," I whisper as my hands trail over his bronze chest plate.

"For what?" he groans, kissing the small horn in the center of my head.

Looking up at him, I smile. "All this time, I thought coming home to Viridia was where I'd find my strength. Little did I know, I'd find more strength and comfort in your arms. You are my home."

"Well then, I should give you a very proper welcome home."

# CHAPTER 38

# *Roark*

The sight of Pella's eyes twinkling as she looks up at me is all I could ever ask. While I still have a litany of questions, there's only one thing on my mind right now.

I need to sink into that pretty little pixie pussy before I fucking combust.

Pella's wings are still covering her, but I need to finally see her in all her glory.

"Spread your wings," I command, my tone harsher than I intend, but Pella doesn't seem to mind.

Slowly, her wings unfold—first the top set, revealing her perfect pair, followed by her second set, showing her svelte waist. But when the third set flutters open and I see the golden fleece of curls tucked into that pretty little *V*, I nearly lose my mind.

I barely have a chance to think before my flesh is melding over bone, strong muscle tethering together, removing every trace of the Reaper. Pella's face softens some as she watches me transform, and her hands quickly find their way to my biceps and along my eight-pack.

A sly grin curves at the corner of her apricot-colored lips when she grabs my holster. I snip the latch on the side, allowing my weapons to fall on the ground while I remove my chest plate and scythe saddle.

Pella's hand smooths over my crotch, and her eyes pop up to me when she feels the rock hard bulge waiting to be released.

"Take him out," I growl, needing to feel her hand on my cock.

Dropping to her knees, Pella pulls down my britches just enough so my girth could lunge out to meet her. I'm hard as an iron door, beads of cum leaking from my crown.

Pella's eyes grow wide in fear as she looks up at me and then back down at my length. "Oh," she gasps, her tiny hands exploring me.

"Do I frighten you?" I bark, desperate to be inside her.

"Well, yes and no," Pella mumbles, dropping her hand from me.

Whatever is wrong, we need to clear the air quickly. "So what about me scares you?"

She looks back at my cock. "Wondering how you plan to fit that inside me."

My shoulders roll in amusement. "Why don't you let me worry about that. In the meantime, you just open that pretty mouth of yours. I need to teach you a lesson about keeping secrets. These lips are mine, and they'll share everything with me because I'm about to share everything with you."

The innocent gaze in her eyes as she looks up at me, her glittery wings fluttering at her back, turns me the fuck on. Taking her hands, I place them over my length.

"There you go, love. Only take as much as you can," I say, encouraging her as I rub my hand through her hair. It's best that she controls this part for now, let her take what she can handle. "Just be sure to swallow, because I'm not wasting a drop."

"Like this?" Pella asks sweetly, kissing the tip as she relaxes her jaw to take me in.

"Good girl," I moan. "Your lips look perfect like this. Make it nice and wet so I can ease into that sweet golden pussy."

She moans around my cock, twirling her tongue around the head and sucking back another inch. She's going deeper than I thought her tiny mouth could take, but I won't stop her.

Reaching down to her side, Pella grabs my scythe. I want to ask what she's doing, but she swirls my dick in her mouth so masterfully, I lose all my thoughts. Clenching my eyes closed, I throw my head back, enjoying the feel of her deep throating me.

Then, I feel something strange.

There's a tingling sensation knocking at my core, making my dick grow harder, expanding in Pella's mouth as she chokes me back. Looking down, I see Pella holding the rod end of my scythe, rubbing it on her clit.

What the fuck?

How did she know?

"Ahh...damn, love," I grit as I feel myself moving toward the edge. "You're a greedy little pixie, aren't you? Fucking drink this down like a good girl. Good girls get Reaper's dick. Is that what you want?" Heady blindness takes over as I bottom out in her mouth.

She moans as I ram myself down her throat until she's gagging, swallowing my cum as golden tears trail down her lovely face. Pella's pretty wings flutter hard as she flicks her pussy back and forth on my scythe until I feel her juices running down my rod.

Never before have I felt anything so good. No one has ever fucked my scythe before, and no one else but Pella ever will.

Pulling out of her mouth, I admire how beautiful she looks with the shadow of my cum running down her chin, but my dick is far from finished. Still holding my massive length, I drop to my knees as Pella falls to her back.

She wastes no time baring it all as she parts her legs, revealing the pretty little thing that has my mind on edge. I want to taste her again, but the way she's reaching out for me tells me how needy she is.

"Please, Roark," she whines, stretching her legs as wide as she can.

I see everything. "Damn, Pella. You want me to fuck this pussy hard, don't you?"

"No!" she shouts, her eyes sparking like lightning, causing me to stop in my tracks. "I want you to reap it—cold, hard, and savage. It's yours!"

"It's gonna hurt, love," I rasp, nudging at her entrance. Her plump folds are warm and wet against my crown, and I yearn to rut through her like a beast, but I hold firm. Instead, I let her adjust to the feel of my crown, breaking through her opening. I need to see how much she can take. "Let me prime you up, make sure you're ready for what I have to give."

She's my delicate, sweet little pixie. I won't hurt her.

Pella lifts her hips some, drawing in another thick inch. "More," she pleads, writhing beneath me.

A man can only take so much, but I continue circling around, stretching her so she can be ready to take me in full. "We're almost there, love," I moan, dipping a little deeper into her slick center.

Reaching to my side, Pella grabs my scythe. "If you don't fuck me, I will," she growls.

Shaking my head, I grunt, shoving her arm back to her side. The scythe thumps hard beside us. "No, no, no," I warn. "You don't put anything in this pussy of mine without my permission. You're my mate now. Soon, this sweet little golden fleece will give itself fully to me. You'll come on this dick. You'll ride it, and then you'll suck it again. Anytime I want this pussy, it will give itself to me. Do you understand?"

Whining, Pella moans, lifting her hips, trying to draw me in, but I pull back.

"Say you understand!" I roar.

"Yes, Roark, please!" she cries out. With her blessing, I drive my steel length so deep into her sweet little hole that we become one.

# CHAPTER 39

# *Pella*

"**H**old onto me, love," Roark whispers against my mouth as he rams himself forward.

With my hands clawing his back, I allow the movement of his rippling muscles to coax my angst as he tears my virginity to shreds, inch by inch.

Sweet tears race down the sides of my face, and I cry out his name while he reaps everything that belongs to him. They're not tears of sadness, but rivers of joy. I've waited more than two times the lifespan of a mortal for this day to come, and now that it's finally here, with this behemoth of a creature who loves me for all that I am, my heart rejoices.

"Almost there," Roark groans, grinding another thick inch inside me.

"See how this little pixie pussy adjusts to me? Because it's mine. Say it," he commands, crashing his mouth to mine.

"It's yours!" I'm mewling, desperate for him to break me apart, to tear me in two. He's the only one capable of putting me back together.

Roaring a series of expletives in the old tongue, Roark pounds my pussy hard, and I belt a note so high, lightning cracks the sky, almost brighter than the sun as it explodes all around us. Golden leaves fall from the Great Oak as the shimmering, misty haze of the garden rests like diamonds upon our skin and the foliage around us.

I've never seen anything so beautiful.

That is, until Roark pulls his face from my neck and looks down at me. There's a radiant glow about him now that wasn't there before. He looks more youthful, and his skin is painted with a faint dusting of gold similar to mine.

Tenderly strumming my face, Roark gazes down at me with a sweet smile that melts my heart. "Are you okay? I didn't hurt you too badly, did I?" he asks, running his hand down the length of me, gently grazing my sex. His eyes travel beneath me to a faint blot of blood on the ground. Growling at the sight of it, his lips curl with a smug satisfaction.

I bite my bottom lip, my lashes fluttering a bit as I feel my cheeks warm. "You hurt me too good," I coo, twirling my fingers through his beard as it hangs over me. "Now I want more," I purr, pulling him in for a quick kiss.

Shaking his head, he lets out a small laugh. "It seems I've created a monster."

My gaze darkens as I lift a brow. "Oh dears," I start, slowly sliding out from under him. Intrigue fills his face as he watches me rise to my knees, my wings piping hard up and down. "Did you think you were the only monster here?"

Growling, Roark's face flashes with his Reaper mode and back to his normal skin, and his eyes darken to black as he watches me drop to all fours. Licking my lips, I shake my hair fully free of my messy bun as my wings stretch out, revealing my whole backside.

"Fuck!" Roark grits, grasping his shaft. "I like watching you crawl for me, especially with that pretty little pussy shining bright, still leaking with my cum."

My eyes flash like lightning, and I let out a small hiss as I crawl, circling around him. "They want my light," I whisper, unleashing a new, sultrier part of me I've never met.

*Well hello,* I say to myself.

"They'll never get it," Roark roars back, his chest heaving hard and fast. My mouth waters as I watch his cock grow even harder, thick, and veiny, with a shiny crown dripping with the shadow of his cum.

Licking my lips, I keep my sights trained on the monster in his grip before looking up at him again. "Aww," I tease, narrowing my eyes and flapping my wings. "Whatever will you do to stop them?"

Before I can circle him again, Roark grabs me by my heels and pulls me back to him. I let out a little scream, but he knows I'm only goading the barbarian in him to come out and play. He's been too civil to me. I need him to know he can have his way with me. He can do anything to me, as long as I end up in his arms.

Grabbing my hips, he lines himself up with my entrance. "Well, let's see what we can do to darken that pretty little soul," he grits out.

"No!" I protest, using my wings to push him back.

But he's not taking no for an answer as he pulls my hips back to him. "What did you just say to me?" he barks, yanking my hair back so I can feel his cool breath brush over me.

"I want the Reaper!" I bite back, wiggling my rear against his hard length.

With a gasp, Roark's grip in my hair lessens. "Hold on, love." His voice is calmer. "Are you serious?"

Once more, my gaze darkens and I even spy concern drifting between Roark's brows as he watches me. "I want the Reaper."

"Love, I don't know if I can control myself if I let him free. I can barely contain myself on my own. I'd hate it if anything happened to you," he says, draping his arms around my shoulder with a gentle pinch of my chin.

But my inner brat is here to stay.

A loose tear falls from my eye as I flutter my lashes up, giving him the sweet, innocent pixie who's had him trying to hide the hard-on he's had since we left the mountains that he didn't think I noticed.

"Please, Roark." I let out another faux tear. "If you don't take it, they'll come for it." I poke out my bottom lip.

Snarling, he roars, grabbing me by my throat. "No one will take what is mine!"

*There he is,* I whisper to myself.

A heavy rumble churns through Roark's chest as his eyes fade to black and his ghastly Reaper form appears. A dark shadow looms around us, and his scythe glows from the ground. He reaches out his hand, and the scythe soars to his waiting palm.

The curved edge of the blade lands at the base of my throat as Roark uses his free skeletal hand to pull my hips back to his waiting girth. There are no sweet words or utterances of affection as he slams into my slick entrance. Nothing but a malevolent chortle rips through him as he plows into me from behind.

This is the Reaper. *My Reaper.* Dangerous. Dark. Everything I never knew I needed.

Every thrust is a death stroke as the scythe teases my throat with my own demise, forcing me to take the grueling punishment I begged for or die resisting.

I don't know how I knew I needed this, but I do. Something in me needed to know I'd die without his love. That he is my home. My deliverance.

Pella is indeed a monster of my own making.

If I didn't stop us, we'd still be going at it. While time works differently in the Netherworld, if we were in the earthbound realm, it would be somewhere around six months of non-stop fucking.

Every time I thought she'd had her fill, she'd find a new way for more. Although I told her we had the rest of our existence to try new positions, Pella insisted on every possible maneuver she could fathom.

She already has her favorites.

Whether it's me behind her, pounding into her until her knees go weak while I hold her wings together, or making love under the moon-flower fountain, Pella's passionate prowess knows no bounds. But she's not alone; I have a few positions that drive me to insanity, but my new favorite is letting her ride me. It's the most dangerous of choices, since she's in complete control and is content to fuck for as long as she'd like, but it's the best angle to enjoy her perfect breasts as they bounce. I also get to taste the sweet honey that drips from her nipples every time she comes. It's perfect.

Pella also finds ways to play into her mischievous pixie charm. Knowing I can't resist the sight of her pussy, she'll often casually open her legs or lift up her rear. Once I see it, I have to fuck it. Even if it means spanking her for making me fuck her, she doesn't care; she'll take her punishment like a good girl or offer to let me empty myself in her mouth.

She is insatiable, and I love it.

I know she fears leaving Viridia. We both know returning to Purgia means keeping our love a secret, at least until we're finally able to confess what we have to Kharon. I know he won't be happy. He could very well end my life because of it, but I do not fear what I already am. *Death*. I do, however, fear any finality without Pella. I want her as my companion in life, death, and everything in between.

I want her always.

Stomping past me, Pella sticks out her tongue before biting into a goldenberry. She's wearing a new set of leaves with a purple silk wrapping. I had the silkworms craft it to cover her rear. I'm not sure if she likes her new frock, but it'll have to do until she finds something else at the Soleil.

"Stop being spoiled." I shoot her a stare. I know she thinks I'll fall for her bratty ways, but I'm keeping my wits about me. The last thing I need is for the Scullards to find us fucking. I won't be at my best, and she'll be too exposed. Besides, I promised her we'd get a good one in after I knew she was safe.

"Hungry?" she fusses, still pouting as she throws two pieces of fruit my way. I know she was trying to hit me with them, but I only laugh as I catch them without looking, and she stomps off, mad she's not getting her way.

"Get over here!" I shout, waving her toward me. "You need to practice some more."

Folding her arms, Pella throws me a hearty eye roll before lifting into the air and landing at my side. "How do you know I haven't been practicing?" she grouses, picking up the bow I made for her.

"I haven't seen you practice," I grunt, positioning myself behind her and offering her an arrow. Pointing at the three pieces of fruit I placed for target practice, I line her up and fix her elbows.

Sighing, Pella notches the arrow. "Please. I could do this with my eyes closed," she snips, cinching her eyes tight.

As she does, I see the one thing my gut told me was coming: the blossoms in bloom.

Bright red blossoms lift from the field around us, signaling danger is near. A faint whistling sound pierces my ear, and I know the dark guard is warning me those mangy beasts are close.

"Pella!" I shout, tapping her shoulder.

"Get off me!" she snaps back, twisting away with her eyes still closed. "I've got this," she says, rearing her arm back to fire off the arrow.

"Pella, down!" I scream, pushing her to the ground as a large beast tears through the nearby gate.

Reaching behind me, I pull out my scythe and rip through the creature with one swift stroke. Another Scullard plunges behind the first, but Pella's arrow hits him square between the eyes, killing him dead.

"Roark!" Pella cries out, opening her eyes to see a raid of Scullards rushing into Viridia.

The garden grows darker as the murky gray skies hover over us. Just as it had when I arrived, the ground shakes and the branches rattle, knowing danger is here.

Still, the Scullards pour into the garden. They're working hard, letting the weaker ones work the gates as the larger use their carcasses as leverage to plow through. These beasts know no honor in life or death, and they shall receive no decency from me or my blade.

It's been far too long since I've reaped, and it feels fucking great to swing my blade again.

Lifting up from the ground, Pella soars above me, firing off round after round of arrows. Damn, she's faster than I thought.

Winking down at me, she gives me a cheeky grin. "Oh, I forgot to tell you," she starts, firing off a few more. "My father taught me to shoot before I grew into my wings." She laughs as she flutters about, still firing arrows.

Raking my scythe through three Scullard in one stroke, I growl at her. "What did I tell you about secrets, Pella of Viridia?" I shove my boot into one of the beast's heads as it falls to the ground.

She fires another arrow. "Then I look forward to my punishment!" she yells at me with a bright smile.

Thrusting my blade through a smaller creature at my side, the sight of a larger one closing in behind Pella turns my earlier irritation into something far darker.

*Rage.*

A dark shadow grows behind me as large, hairy arms grab me from behind. Grizzly, snarling sounds echo in my ear as a husky Scullard jumps from the stone landing to bring me down.

"Come here, you little wench!" he snarls against my ear, licking his slimy tongue down my chin.

"Get your bloody hands off me!" I roar, squirming in his tight hold as we land.

More Scullards crowd around Roark as he swipes his scythe, severing the heads of over a dozen in one stroke, but more continue to pour in.

The sound of blades and fighting from afar tell me the guard is closing in, but they must still be in the fields. Roark needs their help now. I don't know how many he can fend off on his own, but he's showing no signs of recoil.

Squeezing me tighter, the Scullard laughs as he throws me to the ground. Stomping his hoofs into my sternum, he holds me still. Lifting his sword from its sheath, he brandishes it high enough for Roark to see.

"Now watch, Reaper, as I breed this pixie wench," he sneers, letting his long tongue graze his tusks.

"If you touch her, I'll make you long for death," Roark seethes, ripping his scythe through another set of Scullard beasts as he charges toward us, but more beasts crowd him, blocking his view.

Dropping his knickers, the beastly feign reveals his forked, disheveled shaft. It's a grotesque thing and quite small for such a large beast. Looking at him, I can hardly take him seriously. A small chuckle escapes me as I continue staring at the sickly little thing.

"And what do you think you're going to do with that?" I laugh again, pointing at his withered piece.

A few of the nearby beasts snort, looking shamefully away in amusement. Embarrassed, the beast leans over and sears his hand across my face.

"You'll like it plenty when you're screaming," he hisses, dropping to his knees.

"Pella!" Roark shouts, and I see his blade ripping through the herd of Scullards, working hard to get to me.

"All hail Tobin!" one of the nearby Scullards shouts.

"Do her fast and give us a go!" another heckles from afar.

Tobin leans over me, thick saliva seeping between sharp fangs, wickedness waxing the whole of his gaze.

Then, I hear it.

The ground beneath me is not shaking after all. It is the sound of a thousand ancestors calling out to me, a song of strength and power, reminding me who I am.

*I am not weak.*

I am not a pawn of wretched, impotent beings.

I am a Daughter of Viridia. Sacred keeper of the Great Oak. Aide to the High Court of the Great Prince of Purgia. Mate of the Reaper of the Netherworld.

I am me.

With a great shriek, a fury of light shines from the entirety of my being, blinding Tobin and all who stand near. Lifting up from the ground, I fly high above the horde below me—so high, I reach the tip of the massive Great Oak. I hear Roark call me from below, and I zero in on where he stands—not to respond, but just to ensure he is free of my wrath.

Clasping my hands together, I send a small cloud to rest over Roark, shielding him from what comes next. He continues calling my name, but I do not answer. Twirling my wrists, I blow out my pixie dust over the herd surrounding Roark.

In awe, Tobin and his pack shriek in fear as their comrades fade to ash. "Witch!" one calls out, pointing at me.

As I land near Roark, the mist disintegrates, and he too looks at me in shock. Still, he keeps both his scythe and his ax at the ready.

"No," I laugh as a thousand voices echo in kind, bouncing around the garden. "I am no witch," I announce, taking a small step forward as they cower before me, their eyes pinned on the dark cloud hovering over me. "I am a Daughter of Viridia and the mate of the Reaper." I pause, watching as Tobin and a few others make the connection. "I am Pella."

"Make her pay, Tobin," a smaller Scullard gripes, pulling at his arm. "Breed the pixie wench!"

Yanking his arm free, Tobin snarls but steps away from me. Sniffing the air, his eyes roll back into his head. "Her virgin blood's been spilled," he barks as the truth becomes evident.

Scullards can only breed virgins. Thankfully for me, Roark took care of that.

Gasps emanate through the compound as the Scullards skulk back against the gate. But there is no escape—the Dark Guard has them surrounded. Pounding his scythe into the ground, Roark steps forward, ready to end them all.

Placing my hand at Roark's chest, I shake my head. "No, my love," I whisper, lightly grazing my hand across his face. "Your blade shall not be their end."

"Beloved, they cannot be shown an ounce of leniency!" he snarls, his face warping between Roark and Reaper. "At least let my guard finish them."

Still shaking my head, I offer him a small smile. "No," I murmur.

Backing up, Tobin and the remaining Scullard horde plow toward the gate, but the Dark Guard maintains their place. "We'll leave you be," Tobin clamors, stumbling backward.

"Oh dears," I say sweetly, clasping my hands beneath my chin. "You didn't think I was going to let you leave here alive, did you?" I let out a maniacal giggle. "Oh, Nethers no!" My voice drops an octave. "You owe Viridia a debt, and it will be repaid. In blood."

A blinding light glows around me as my wings burst into flames. Lifting my arms in the air, I swirl my wrist around, beckoning the leaves to do my will. They crackle and burst into bombs of fire, falling over Tobin and the remaining herd within the gate.

Screams echo through the garden as the Scullards ashen husks fall to the ground. A few stragglers run off, chased by the guard, and a handful flee the guards entirely, but there is one thing I know from this day forward: Scullards will never return to Viridia again.

TALE

GR

&  RE

S OF

M

PER

**P**ella is singing again.

Actually, she sings all the time now. Ever since she defeated the Scullards back in Viridia, all she does is sing.

She enchanted me with her song while I fucked her one last time before we left her homeland, belting high notes at every pit stop when I plowed deep into her on our way back to Purgia.

Now, here she is, riding me, her head tilted and her back arched, singing like a siren to my soul. The notes she hits as she climaxes are almost as amazing as how beautiful she looks with her wings outstretched, shimmering gold when she calls out my name.

We've stayed hidden in my lair since we've returned. No one ever comes here, and my guard knows to alert me when someone is near.

I just can't pull myself away from her.

"Mmm…" Pella moans, crashing her head onto my chest. She's still pulsing around my length, quaking in my arms as she settles from her orgasm. "I'll never tire of this," she coos, running her small fingers through my beard.

I plant a kiss on her forehead. "And I'll never tire of loving you, or this sweet pussy," I growl, squeezing her rear. "I love you, woman," I grin, tightening my hold, rolling us side to side.

Giggling, Pella pounds her tiny fists into my chest. "Roark!" she squeals, still laughing.

"Say it back, or I'm not letting you go!" I tease, tapping my fingers along the seam of her wings.

"Oh Roark, please don't!" she quips, knowing I'll hit the spot that'll have her laughing for hours.

"You better say it!" I growl, strumming my fingers up and down.

"I love you!" Pella finally admits, joyful tears racing down her face as she folds into me. Beating my chest again, she tries to wiggle out of my hold. "You know I do, you big brute!"

Lifting her face to mine, I give her a stare. "There's nothing like hearing it from your lips."

Shaking her head, she throws me a sly eye roll. "And there's nothing like having my barbarian of a mate lavish affection on me until he gets what he wants."

"You like it rough, eh?" I smile, watching Pella give a bashful nod. Groaning into the nape of her neck, I take a hard whiff of her sweet scent. "I always get what I want, love."

"And what is it that you want now, my lord?" Pella asks as her hands stroke my length.

The want seeping from her now is pushing me to the precipice. Pella has an insatiable appetite for sex, and if it were up to her, that's all we'd do. In fact, that's all we've done since we've come back to Purgia. I've barely reaped since my return, save a dozen or so vagrants I found wandering the fields near my lair. Who knows how many more are out there wandering? I'll never know if we continue at this rate. It's enough that I'll have to find a way to confess my affection for Pella to Prince Kharon when he returns. The last thing I need is for the city to be overrun because I've slacked on my duties.

But maybe we can spare a little time.

"I want you to make my bed rock," I answer, my tone hard and dark.

Pella's shoulders shrug as her cheeks flush. "How?"

"Come sit on my face, that's how." My voice is even harsher as I lift her up by her waist.

"Roa–" she purrs as I cover my mouth over her sweet golden pussy.

Now, she's singing again.

~

**P**ella's sleeping peacefully—she always does after I feast on her like a starved caveman. I'm not sure if it's the multiple orgasms or that she floods my beard like a river, but my beloved is always done for when I eat her out.

The look of peace on her face as her small body lays nestled in my bed makes me the happiest creature in all the Netherworld.

Pella made the most adorable grunt as I whispered in her ear that I was stepping out to reap, and my soul did a little jig of its own, admiring the lovely creature in my bed.

It feels good to be out in the fields again. Leaning against my footwall, I've reaped fifty or so souls in the short time I've been out here.

Seems like more than my usual body count, but the number of vagrants seeking to evade the ships to the Underworld are at an all-time high. Sometimes, I wonder if they actually think they can lurk outside the walls of Purgia without being caught, or if they waltz into my path with every intention of ending their meaningless lives.

Whatever the case, I am more than happy to give them a fitting end.

"My lord Reaper!" a loud voice calls to me from the top of the overlook.

Turning around, I peer beneath my hand and notice Gao's stout form waving at me.

"Gao?" I say, surprised to see him near my lair. No one ever comes here, not unless they seek a reaping.

Trotting down the hill, Gao's round frame topples side to side down the rocky terrain. "My lord!" he shouts again with an erratic twirl of his wrist. He's mumbling something, but it's hard to hear. I look up to see the leads of the dark guard just behind him. The fact they let him through tells me this must be urgent.

Offering my hand to help Gao down the rest of the way, I wait for him to catch his breath. "What is it, Gao?"

"My, am I glad to see you, my lord. Had Oru not spotted your guard, I thought we'd be lost!" Gao rattles as he wipes his balding scalp with worry.

"What do you mean, old man?" I grumble.

"We thought you were still away with Pella, but seeing your guard, I knew the Fates sent you back just in time."

Sighing, I shake my head. He's rambling, and I don't have the energy to discern his intent. "Watch out!" I grit out as a straggler wanders by. Shoving Gao behind me, I wrench my scythe through a lanky, decrepit-looking creature. He reminds me of a gryphon, but not entirely. His soulless eyes tell me all I need to know: he's due for the Underworld but has chosen vagrancy instead. Now that Fate has led him to my door, his reaping will be his finality.

"Oh my–oh my!" Gao groans behind me. "It's already started, I'm afraid."

Turning around, I give Gao a look while still holding the creature in mid-air. "What has started?"

"Why, my lord, it's the eve of Festivus!" Gao exclaims, his wide gaze full of both excitement and trepidation.

Fuck! That explains why there are so many vagrants roaming about.

Growling, I fling the creature off my blade into the pile at my footwall. I can't believe how off I am.

Taking a deep breath, I try to quiet the warring in my gut. "Okay, where is the Grim lord?"

"That's just it, sire. The Grim lord's been a bit too heavy on the mead since your departure. In fact, Sabine said he's still at the Grave Tavern as we speak."

"You can't be serious," I seethe, my jaws clenched tight.

"I'm afraid so, my lord," Gao huffs, wiping his scalp once more. "I do apologize for the intrusion, but I had nowhere else to turn. Nethers knows

I'm thankful you've returned. And about that–how did Pella fare? The Great Prince will be looking for her when he comes to the citadel."

My brow lifts. "The Great Prince?" I take another breath. I hope he's not saying what I think he is.

"Oh yes, my lord Reaper," Gao continues, his face brightening to a smile. "The henches spotted his ferry not far off from shore. Of course Prince Kharon wouldn't miss Festivus!" Gao happily exclaims as I shove him forward.

"Well, thanks for coming by, Gao," I say, pushing him toward the lower gate. It's a better path than the hill he climbed to get here. "I should get to the Grim lord, make sure everything is ready for the prince's arrival."

Nodding in agreement, Gao saunters through the gate. "Yes, yes, best make sure the Grim lord is fit to greet Prince Kharon upon his arrival. Finally, some semblance of order around here," he grumbles on his way out. Turning quickly on his heel, he lifts a finger. "By the way, you never said what happened to Pella. Is she safe?"

A dark smile crowds the side of my face as my eyes darken. "Yes, Gao. Pella couldn't be safer."

# CHAPTER 43

# Pella

"Pella!" Roark roars, waking me from my slumber.

Rolling over, I yawn; I'd much rather keep sleeping. "What?" I murmur, cramming my head into the pillow.

"Get up! We've got to go! Now!" he roars, shaking the foot of his massive poster bed.

Jumping up, I rub my eyes, still trying to get my bearings. Nothing but panic and dread mars Roark's perfect face. His thick brows crowd together at the center of his forehead, and his lips are drawn into a line so tight, I can barely make them out under his wooly beard and mustache.

"What's wrong?" I whisper, fearing what he'll say next.

"It's Festivus Eve!" he barks as he grabs my frock and tosses it to me.

My heart races, knowing it's the biggest time of the season for the Netherworld.

"Oh, okay," I say, quickly standing to pull my legs through my attire. "Well, I'll get back to the palace and help with—"

"And Kharon's back," Roark blurts, his voice rippling with strained notes of dread.

Gasping, I drop the side strings of my frock and cover my mouth. Since we've returned to Purgia, Roark and I have been in our own world, loving and existing as though nothing and no one else mattered. Festivus is one thing, but Kharon's return is something else entirely.

"But–but–we–how—" My words are garbled; I can hardly think.

Scooping me up in his arms, Roark settles me over his waist. "Shh…" He quiets my worry with the gentle touch of his finger over my mouth and his cool breath upon my skin. Gently running his hands through my hair, he pulls a few loose strands away from my face. "No worries, love," he whispers, leaning his forehead to mine. "Everything will work out just as it should."

"How can you say that?" I mutter, tears filling my eyes. "Once the prince knows about us, he will—"

"Understand," Roark adds, finishing my sentiment. My eyes pop up to his, a lone tear falling down my cheek. "I've never believed in fate until you came into my life. Now that I have you, I have to believe what we have was written in brimstone, marred in fire and ash, deep in the hollow of this world. All we have to do is trace our footprints in its ashes.'"

More tears flow from my eyes, making it hard to see. Still, I can make out the enchanting dark hollow of his eyes and the sweep of his mustache over his lips. "Walk in the ashes, huh?" I whisper, lightly twining my fingers through his beard.

"You ready to walk in the ashes with me, love?" He breathes, adding a small kiss to my lips. I can still smell a hint of my pussy on his mouth, and the memory of what we shared lifts my spirits.

"Over fire and ash," I giggle, pressing my mouth to his once more.

Lifting my arms, Roark slides the strings over my shoulders and tightens the strap at my back. Sometimes, I feel like such a doll in his arms when he dotes on me like this.

"Gao also told me Thelios is taken to drunkenness."

I adjust the leaves around my waist, fluttering my wings to settle into my clothes. I've been naked for so long, wearing this frock feels foreign.

"Really? That doesn't sound like him."

Sighing, Roark pulls me back in his arms. "I suppose I shouldn't have suggested he drink away his cares after losing the Specter."

"What!" I shriek, jumping back some. "When?"

Frowning, Roark gives me a look. "Oh, love, I thought you knew. It happened when the Scullards came into the Soleil. Maybe it was after they took you."

Pursing my lips together, I replay my memories of the Scullard attack. The last time I saw Sydney, she was going after Amarok. Then again, I was taken around the same time, so I may have missed it.

"Poor Sydney," I whisper, saddened by the news. "And Hala!" I shout, thinking of her sister.

Roark doesn't seem as bothered by the news as he is irritated. "We can worry about them later. For now, we need to get Thelios together so he can facilitate today's events and be at his best to welcome the prince. Once Festivus is over, we can check on Hala. Besides, I'm sure she is safe with Liv. Our only focus should be ensuring the prince's comfort. That's the only way we can set him at ease when we share our news."

Shaking my head, I quietly agree.

"Come here," Roark growls, pulling me back to him. "I love you, woman," he barks into my hair as he lifts me around his waist.

My wings flutter hard against my back as a wide smile covers my face. "I love you too," I confess, enjoying the feel of his bulking arms around me.

Roark's eyes dance like he just struck gold as he glares back at me, but he's not the only lucky one. Pressing his lips to mine, Roark kisses me like it's the last time.

Perhaps it is.

"Will someone please bring me the nightshade!" Sabine yells, throwing a canister across the tavern. "And fill it up! The Grim lord needs all he can get."

"Play the song again!" I chuckle, lifting a small, bearded troll in my arms and twirling her around. "I am dancing with my queen!" I smile, pulling the troll into my embrace.

Struggling against my chest, the troll mashes her hands against my chin. "My lord, please!" she quips, working hard to free herself.

"Please?" I coo, resting my forehead against hers. "Please for another go? Why, of course!" I yelp, lifting her high and twirling her fast.

Her eyes bulge, and her brunette beard sways in the wind we create at our spin. She is a delight. I know what and who she is; there is no pretense, save whatever may be living under that mountainous mane against her chin. What I see is what I get.

"My lord, put her down!" Sabine calls to me from behind. I hear the sound of liquid being poured into something behind me, but I don't turn around. "Faster, you idiot!" she barks at someone, but I don't bother to turn around.

"Oh, no, this one and I are to be mated!" I jovially cry out. "At least this one cannot deceive me. Can you, love?" I mewl in a sing-song tone, pressing my forehead to hers.

A loud roaring sound rises behind me, and the eyes of the troll widen in alarm.

"Get your hands off my wife!" a thunderous voice calls to me from below. Looking down, I see a stout yet short bearded troll standing on a stool at the bar.

"Your wife?" I sneer, looking at the damsel in my arms and twirling her around once more. "You must be mistaken, good sir. This fair one is hand-picked to be my bride. And what a pair we'll make! Wouldn't you say so, Sabine?"

"My lord, please drink this!" Sabine snips, handing me a steaming cup of something that smells horrid.

Swatting her hand away, I turn back to the bard, gesturing he continue with his song.

"You'll take your hands off her, or I will—" the troll roars aloud, jumping up from the stool with a serving tray in his hand.

Covering the troll at my side with my arm, I turn my back to the grumbling one, hopeful to take the brunt of his attack. I'm surprised when I feel nothing—nothing, that is, except a looming presence behind me.

"Ah, I'll take this," I hear a familiar voice say.

Turning around, I'm surprised to find Roark towering over me, holding the grumbling troll by the wrist in the air.

"Old friend!" I squeal, throwing my arms around Roark's waist. I've never been happier to see him than I am now.

The bearded damsel at my side stumbles back toward Sabine, seemingly thankful to be free of my hold. The troll in Roark's grip glares at me like he wished to say something, but being manhandled by such a large, domineering creature such as Roark would put anyone at a loss for words.

"Put him down!" I hear a tiny, buzzing voice squeal at Roark's side. I'm surprised to see Pella fluttering over Roark's shoulder.

"Pella!" I shriek, actually happy to see her. "You're here! And in one piece. My, am I glad the Scullards didn't eat you alive. That would have been a terrible fate."

Pella's nose crinkles some as I speak, and she covers her face. Shaking her head in agreement, she flutters back to Roark's shoulder. "Yes, my lord. I am very fortunate," she says. Looking up at Roark, she bobs her head to the side, motioning for him to put down the troll.

Roark's chest rumbles a bit. "Best get a move on," Roark sneers toward the troll and my dance partner as he releases him. "You don't want to miss the festivities." Knocking his head to one side, he gestures toward the door as both trolls run out, hand in hand from our view.

"But I was to marry her!" I whine, pressing toward the door.

"Oh, no you don't, my friend," Roark grouses, a heavy hand at my chest. "Not without this," he orders, offering me the same stench-ridden bog Sabine offered.

Turning my head, I fold my arms across my chest. "I think not!"

"Mmm..." Roark grumbles, lifting me in the air and throwing me against the pub table. "Looks like we'll have to do this the hard way. Pella, hold his nose. Sabine, his arms."

Before I have a chance to protest, Roark is pouring heaps of Nightshade down my throat. The scalding hot liquid burns through me like lava, melting everything in its wake. Screaming, I choke out two whiffs of fire like a dragon before rolling over on my side in agony.

Patting my back hard, Roark laughs haughtily as I exhale heaps of soot from my lungs. "That's it, my lord. Get it all out."

Shaking his heavy hand off me, I climb down from the table, leaning between two stools. "I'm fine! I'm fine!" I shout as my head pounds from drunkenness.

Settling to my feet, thoughts of my adventures as of late are quite disarming. From dancing with that grotesque troll to practically wallowing in the mirth stains I left at the Soleil, lamenting over my loss of Sydney, I've been a fool.

"How long have I been like this?" I mutter, holding my head, trying to make sense of it all.

"Long enough that you needed Nightshade to bring you down," Sabine says with her arms folded.

Locking his large palm onto my shoulder, Roark gives me a stare. "Are you well, my lord?" Shaking my head as my only reply, I offer a faint smile. "I do hope so, because it is now the eve of Festivus."

I bolt upright, my eyes popping open. "What?" I shriek in horror.

"Yes, old friend. The henches have spotted the Ferryman closing in," Roark continues, squeezing my shoulder tight.

Throwing his hand off my shoulder, I press by him and Sabine. "Then what the bloody hell are we doing standing by? We've got work to do!"

Sabine and Roark trade knowing glances as Pella buzzes between them. There's a strange look of glee on their faces, like they're actually happy to see me. For a moment, I want to share in this sordid reunion, but I can't. Between Festivus and the prince's arrival, there's too much left to do. Besides, if they truly knew what I did to Sydney, they'd hate me, and rightfully so.

"**M**y lords!" Dane shouts from the threshold of the tavern. "The Ferryman is docking!"

"Let's get a move on!" I grunt, making my way to the door.

"My lord Reaper," Dane continues, standing in the way of our exit. "The vagrants," he says, almost out of breath as he holds himself up against the door-frame. "They're everywhere! Roaming throughout the streets like vermin."

"Shit!" I roar aloud, pushing past Dane. "I need to take care of this!" I huff, looking over my shoulder to Thelios.

"Go!" he snips, swiping his hand through the air. "I'll see to the prince's arrival. Pella, you look after the palace. Sabine, curate a grouping for his majesty's harem. I'm sure after being with mortals for so long, His Highness could use proper company."

I shoot Pella a quick glance, hopeful Thelios doesn't notice the way my eyes caress every inch of her from afar. I know I'm not doing a good job of hiding my feelings for Pella; I need to work on doing a better job in front of the prince.

Everyone nods, and then we're off.

~

Normally, I'd see to the prince's arrival, but I need to get rid of the vagrants. Having the streets of Purgia overrun is the last thing Prince Kharon needs to see when he arrives.

Creatures who aren't afforded a place in the lottery of the Grim lord turn into hollowed, zombie-like beings should they try to hide from the ships to the Underworld. Although they're not harmful per se, no one wants to see such decrepit, lost souls wandering the streets of Purgia. Our city might be purgatory, but it is not the Great Prince's aim that we should look the part.

Festivus is a high time of celebration, where those elected to remain in Purgia, avoiding the hand of Hades, dance through the streets, thankful for their pardon.

So, here I stand, doing what I do best. *Tis the season*, I always say. It's Reaping Season!

~

**Thelios**

The prince is here. Finally.

He's settled into his throne nicely. There's an apt smile laced across his face I've never seen before, though I'm sure it has more to do with the petite mortal at his side than being back in the Netherworld.

It's been far too long since he went away—almost ten earthbound years, if I had to guess. Time moves slower here, so it's only been a few months or so from our watch, but his absence is hard to miss.

I'm just glad Pella helped put things back in order around the palace while I've kept him busy going through Tributes for Festivus. It's time for him to choose those he wishes to remain in his court.

Prince Kharon, however, seems more interested to move on from Festivus so he can see to securing his sister's freedom. His whole reason to go to the earthbound plane was to gather what he needed to rescue his sister, Moirai. Now that he's returned, he's set his course toward snatching her from the clutches of the wicked Changelings at all costs.

However, we've been bombarded with unsolicited visitors like the High Serpent Queen and Persephone. The Great Prince has been on edge since their arrival—between wanting to get to his sister while also trying to keep a tight watch on his beloved mortal, Rae, he's been on edge.

From the way the prince watches Rae, like he'd strike even a speck of dirt threatening her very existence, to the way she stays glued to his side, it's obvious she is here to stay.

How he plans to have any relationship with a mortal is beyond me, but to bring her to the Netherworld seems rather reckless. I mean, if he cares so much for her, why bring her here? Danger lurks upon every crevice, and there is no pity of grace to be found, even for someone as lovely as Rae.

But perhaps, that's what love is: reckless, a gondola traipsing over the savagery this world inflicts with nothing but a mere string of hope to carry you along the way.

And that's what I have lost: hope.

The hope I once had is gone. It left when I swallowed Sydney in my mirth, buried in the abyss of my fears.

Throwing back a quick sip of brandy wine, I chug down the bitter liquid, hopeful to douse the ache I feel watching Prince Kharon and Rae fawn over one another. It's quite exhausting, to say the least, but the strange vibes I'm getting from Roark and Pella are equally as nauseating.

Which is why I'm glad he'll be leaving soon.

Although I know it won't be a joyful excursion, I'm looking forward to drowning myself in my own sorrows when the Great Prince and Roark leave to retrieve the prince's sister from *Men-An-Tol*.

Pella has been ordered to keep Rae company while I see to things here at the palace, as per usual. No doubt the prince has noticed I've been drinking more than usual, hence why he's leaving me here. I'll be of little use to him in my condition.

But what other condition could a creature in my position be in? I've not only committed a blasphemous act in having an intimate relationship with my own kin, but a part of me knows if I had to do it all over again, I'd make the same choice.

I fucking love Lorna Sydney, with every part of my damned and wretched soul.

Yet, for as damned and wretched as it is, I do not know how to love.

Love doesn't throw love aside, nor does love cast itself away into oblivion, and that's what I have done. So, what other recourse have I but to indulge in mead and spirits until my soul withers into a hollow grave of its own making?

For that is what I plan to do: await my own desiccation until I am covered in fire and ash and my soul withers like the bruised flower I once gave my heart.

The prince's sister has been saved.

Despite every disadvantage set against us by the Changelings, Moirai is now reunited with her brother, the Great Prince of Purgia. Now, the Great Prince can finally enjoy Festivus.

We've all returned to the High Court of Prince Kharon, and the palace is abuzz with the joy of Festivus and the prince's return from the earthbound plane.

With his mate, Rae, aptly placed at his side, Prince Kharon's smile stretches from ear to ear. Now that his sister, Moirai, Great Fate of the Netherworld, has returned, the Prince appears more jovial than I've seen him in a centuries.

Still, I wish I could share in his glee.

I wish with everything in me that I could cry aloud my heart's desires for Pella, but such things are forbidden. Even with so much fair news ringing about the High Court, I fear sharing my affection for Pella would sully the prince's good mood.

While we've done our best to cover not only Thelios' drinking, but the vagrancy of souls wandering Purgia, only time will tell what else the prince has noticed since his return.

Even Thelios is doing his best to look the part, two damsels on his arm as he strides through the High Court, hoping to appear as normal as possible. Yet, for the life of me, I can hardly set my jaw in a smile at the announcement of Prince Kharon's joyous plans to wed Rae.

Everyone claps, offering congratulations, but none louder than Thelios, who whistles his congrats. "I knew from the moment I saw you two together that she was more than a damsel. I knew she was your mate—but your wife? It does me good to see you happy, sire."

*Fucking suck-up,* I hiss under my breath. It's clear he's been drinking again, but the prince doesn't seem to notice. Pella stomps her heel into my shoulder, giving me a look.

"Thank you, Thelios," Prince Kharon says with a wide smile as he brushes his blonde tendrils behind his ear.

Rae nods in agreement, her warm bright smile and fiery bronze hair aglow as she shares a quaint kiss with the prince.

"Yes," I choke out as Pella shoves her heel into my shoulder once more. "We are all very happy for you indeed," I manage, clenching my teeth at the feel of Pella's heel digging into my flesh.

With a gentle smile at Rae, Prince Kharon takes a step down the staircase. "Roark, is there something you want to say?" Lifting his brow, I see how quickly his mood is changing as his stormy gray eyes lock with mine. "Anything you care to share before my court?" he groans.

Lowering my eyes lest they betray me, I bow my head. "No, my prince," I mumble. I feel Pella crowd closer to my neck, likely wary of the prince's haunting gaze.

Pacing the riser, Kharon folds his arms behind his back. "Many of you may not know this, but when Lady Vereen and I fell in love, we had to hide our feelings. I had to feign interest in someone else, and Rae had to act as though she despised me. Then, she went against her entire family and even her own sensibilities to confess her feelings for me. From that day forward, we loved one another in secret, but never publicly. All of that changes now—not only here in the Netherworld, but when we return to her realm." Pausing, the prince shares a sweet smile with Rae. "It's for that reason I refuse to allow anyone under my hand to bear the weight of love in secret. It is too great a weight to bear."

My stomach churns, a knot welling in my throat as Rae ventures to the prince's side.

"That is why, from this moment forward, I declare that the Grand Reaper of Purgia and the last daughter of Viridia may pursue their love without the weight of secrecy."

How did he know? I share a look with Pella, whose eyes are misty pools of gold.

Gasps echo through the hall as everyone stares at me and Pella. Pella stands up on my shoulder, jumping and clapping her hands.

"Well, damn," Thelios breathes, clasping his chest.

Quickly dropping to my knees, I stretch out my hand before my prince. "Your Highness, it was never my intention to set a course against you," I confess, sighing as a weight lifts from my shoulders.

≈

## Pella

My heart is bubbling with joy. I'm not sure how Prince Kharon figured it out, but Nethers knows I'm glad he did.

Motioning for Roark to rise, Prince Kharon pats his shoulder. His eyes dance between me and Raork, and my wings tell of my joy while fluttering rapidly at my back.

"The sails of love chart their own course, my friend, and it is a course you must take–you, that is, and Pella," Prince Kharon says with a kind smile that reaches his eyes. Leaning toward Roark's shoulder so only we can hear, he continues. "I'll let you two decide when or if you show your true form."

Clapping my hands as my wings flap hard, I turn to Roark.

Roark's eyes glimmer with more hope than I've ever seen. With a quaint shrug of his shoulders, he nods toward me. "It's up to you."

Running off Roark's shoulder, I burst into a ball of light, revealing my true form for the first time to the entirety of the High Court. Murmurs echo throughout the court as I twirl with excitement.

"What the fu—" Thelios blows out an air of shock.

Smiling at me, Prince Kharon narrows his gaze some. "Pella, you may showcase your true form in this castle and within the walls of your own solarium. Outside of the castle gates, I'd like you to remain careful. Of course, you have Roark to keep you safe," he states.

Roark wraps his arm around me as I nestle into his chest, shooting Rae a wink. It's going to be nice having her around—just her presence has changed the prince's normally staunch and stubborn mood.

Moirai stands, taking a step down to her brother's side. "As it has always been, the privacy of this court is without exclusion. Breathing a word of what happens here is tantamount to treason."

My heart stills with the weight of Moirai's charge. Knowing those assembled are ordered to secrecy gives Roark and I all the assurance we need to know I should be safe.

# CHAPTER 47

*Thelios*

I am happy for Roark.

Hell, I'm even happy for the prince.

How everyone around me has been afforded such a grace as love is beyond me.

The Ferryman, the Reaper, both now indebted to love's vices. Yet, here I am, indebted to none.

Now, everyone is gone.

From the looks of it, both the Great Prince and the Reaper are off celebrating with their beloved in whatever way seems fitting. Even Gao and his wife Oru strolled out of the High Court hand-in-hand, twinkles in their eyes.

Then, there's me. The wretch made of mire with no heart.

I didn't even have the heart to show much interest in the damsels Sabine courted for me. There's hardly enough mead in this world or the next to melt the memory of Sydney to be with anyone else. That's why I sent the damsels to Sabine. She has far better use for them than I.

So, here I sit, alone in the High Court, twirling my scythe around in my hand. The coolness of the marble floor is nothing compared to the tepid waters of my soul as I lean against the tall, ornate columns at my back.

For the first time, it's quiet in the High Court, quieter than it's been since Festivus. I believe I heard Rae compare it to the lull mortals feel once the pomp and circumstance of Christmas comes to a screeching halt.

It's been what feels like months of excruciating detail for it to all end so abruptly. From the drawing of lotteries, to executing judgments, to the ordering of Tributes, being the keeper of Festivus is quite an exhausting ordeal.

And without Sydney, it all feels worthless.

"Grim lord!" a small voice calls to me from the shadows. "Why do you sit alone?"

Peering through the darkness, I'm surprised when I see Moirai taking graceful steps back into the grand hall.

"My lady." I jump to my feet, offering a reverent bow. She may not bear the title of princess, but as Lead Regent of the Fates, she is due my respect.

"Please." She waves a hand as she saunters quietly through the hall, her feet barely scraping the cold floor. Moirai is a splendor all her own. With golden, sun-kissed tresses and sparkling eyes like diamonds, her shining silhouette lights up the darkened space. "Now tell me, why do you sit alone?"

Letting out a faux chortle, I steady myself with my scythe, securing my rod to the floor. "Oh, not to worry, my lady. I'm merely resting after more than a full night's watch of Festivus. It's gotten the best of me, I'm afraid."

"I see." She offers a small smile as her eyes examine me. "And what of the one you cast aside? Has she also gotten the best of you?" Moirai says, her blinding gaze burrowing through my soul.

Turning away, lest she see more than I care to share, I make my way toward the exit. "It's best I settle in. Planning for the next season will be here before I know it."

A bright, white light shoots through the darkness, halting my exit. Covering my eyes, I try to press forward, only to find Moirai standing before me.

"And should the next season come, what will be of your heart and that which you have cast aside?"

Fine. If she wants the truth, then she'll hear it. I know what I have done is blasphemous, but if she's intent on hearing me say it, so be it.

"Whatever I've cast aside was not meant to be. I may be of mire, but I'll not settle the whole of the Netherworld into oblivion to suit my needs, no matter how grim they may be."

Moirai's eyes narrow for a moment, and then she smiles. Stepping aside, she resigns to let me pass. "I suppose your needs are grimly still," she whispers as I skulk by. "Then again, all Grim kind are not kin, whether it be cast aside or not, no matter what the legends say."

My feet lock in place, and the coldness from the floor creeps up my spine. "What?" I lash, whipping my head over my shoulder.

Laughing, Moirai continues down the darkened hall, her hands clasped at her waist. I must know more, and my shadows seem just as curious as they carry me to her side.

Dropping to my knee, I bow my head. "My lady Moirai," I chatter, wholly rattled. "Please, I know Fates are not to speak plainly, but I must know."

Her small hand draws up my chin so that I meet her bright gaze. "Dear one, only that which is hidden is meant to be revealed. Such is the story of the Grim. Long ago, when Hades sought power more than anything, he set a crusade against all grim-kind. In his tyranny, he conquered all the lands to bring about the Underworld. Obliterating every creature who stood against him, he left only one remaining Grim line: the young one, unopposed to his will. As such, he ensured no other league of Grim would rise against him. However, unbeknownst to him, there remained another line untouched. His wife, the Queen of the Underworld, Persephone, would see to it that her husband not gain omnipotence. She knew that if he did, his cruelty would know no bounds. So, she gathered the remaining

Grim lines with other cast offs, like Specters, thus starting a new line not marred by the same Grim soil."

Pawing at my face, I cry into my hand. I think nothing of how foolish I look in front of Moirai; all I can think about is what I've done to Sydney, how I cast her into my mirth because I thought we were kin. We are not, and now here I am, all alone.

"What have I done?" I sob, crouching on the floor.

There's a small pat on my head, and I can sense Moirai's pity. "All is not lost, dear one," she whispers in my ear.

"I sent her away!" I groan, banging against the floor with my fist. "Damn it!"

"And only you can go where you sent her," Moirai breathes once more against my ear.

Clawing myself up from the floor, I wipe my eyes. "How–" I tearfully look up, surprised to find myself alone.

*Only you can go where you sent her...* I still hear Moirai's voice echoing around me.

Closing my eyes, I roar as I bang my scythe on the ground. It's time I go to Sydney.

**D**arkness swirls around me as I walk through the mire of my own making.

It's cold, dark, and void of anything resembling life. All I see is darkness, what I see when my more grimly, hollowed state takes over.

There's a looming shadow of loneliness hovering about, and I wonder if this is how it is for all Netherfolk who enter my mirth. The thought makes me sad, but only when I think of Sydney bearing such a fate.

"Sydney!" I call her name as I traipse through the darkness, but nothing—not an echo or response. Just dead silence.

Once more, I call her name, but I hear nothing.

My heart wanders a bit, fearing that perhaps I only imagined my talk with Moirai. I was, after all, left cowering alone on the cold floor. Maybe I'd had more than my share of stiff drinks. That is quite possible.

"Syd–"

"Get out," a dry, hard voice groans from afar.

Turning about, I look for someone, anyone, but I don't see a soul.

"Syd–" I try again, but a strong gale knocks me off my feet into the cold, wet mire beneath me.

"Go!" a thunderous, almost familiar voice shouts.

I look around again, but I don't see anyone—only *something*. A shadowy presence stands a great distance from me, and I can't make it out, but I push myself up from the floor and move closer.

"Leave this place!" an echo of whispers whirl around me, but I am unafraid. "Get out!" the same voice whirls around the darkened space.

"Not until you show your face!" I growl back. I just need to know if I'm in the right place. If this is just some sordid soul looking for revenge, they'll find much worse should they challenge me further.

"Tell me... tell me... *tell me*..." The familiar sound bounces around me. "What sweet offerings *shall you render*... to see my face?" they roar at me, sending another gale my way. This one doesn't catch me by surprise like the first, and I maintain my footing.

"Tell me who you are!" I demand, thrashing the rod of my scythe against the floor.

A hard kick at my back knocks me off my feet. "You first!" This time, I can make out the voice in full.

Flipping over, I jump up and grab the wraith-like creature hovering over me. "Sydney!" I shout. Sneering, the wraith pushes me back as a shadowy flume swirls around us. Shouting Sydney's name once more, I press through the dark mist.

"Stay back!" I hear her voice clearly this time.

"Sydney, please," I beg, my palms raised in surrender. "If you would just let me explain."

"Oh Nethers no, my dear," she sneers, lunging toward me, still hooded in her cloak—except this time, I cannot see any part of her face. "You'll find no pity here," she snarls, whipping around me.

"Using my words against me, eh?" I force a laugh. "At least you remember them!" I call out, reaching inside and snatching Sydney by the wrist.

"Take your hands off me!" She barks, shoving me away.

"I deserve that," I admit, taking another step forward.

Laughing, echoes of her voice coil around me once more. "Oh, it's not merely half of what you deserve."

"Please, Syd," I continue. "I only came to apologize and to take you back to Hala."

The gales simmer to reveal Sydney standing in the middle of the dark, still shrouded in her cloak, and I'm thankful to make out her familiar shadow framing my view.

"I'm waiting," she harshly calls back. Her tone is colder than I recall, but wholly deserving.

"I see things clearer than I did before; it was wrong of me to banish you into my mirth. Even if the truth had not been revealed to me, my actions, as they were, were wrong. For that, I am sorry."

A gust of wind whirls around me, nearly lifting me off my feet, but I hold my ground.

"What truth?" she whispers, barely audible.

"You are not my kin," I yell back, noticing her shadow growing dim. "I thought you were, and that we—I mean, I—had committed an unspeakable act."

The wind whips by me once more. "And to be with me is unspeakable?" she snarls, this time closer.

"No, Syd. I was wrong," I confess, reaching out to touch her, but she backs away into the shadowy mist.

"Wrong for being with me?" Her voice bounces behind me.

I turn about, looking for her. "No!" I still don't see her, but I can feel her. She's close. "No, Sydney," I begin as a lone tear races to my chin. "I was wrong for letting you go, for not telling you the truth of how I felt. Instead, I banished you–"

"Why?" Sydney roars back. "Why did you banish me into your mirth?"

"Because—because—"

"Say it!" she demands, and a strong wind stabs my chest like a knife.

"I–I– thought we were kin–"

Another blow lands, this time to my face. "Liar!" Sydney shrieks, and once more, echoes stir around me. "For once, admit it! Tell me the truth or leave!"

My skin crawls, and a prickling coldness crawls up my spine, but I can no longer run from the truth and she knows it.

Fuck it. "I sent you here because I feared I didn't care if you were my kin—that what I felt for you, I would not deny if I had to look at you, be with you or near you. That I'd let the world fall into oblivion because I wanted you always. I feared what that meant. So, I sent you here."

**R**elief washes over me at his words.

For long days and untold nights, I wandered through the depths of this abyss, wondering if it were only the makings of my own mind that would conjure something I faintly hoped to be true. Now, upon hearing him say it, my soul is finally relieved.

But I am not done with him yet.

"That still doesn't explain why you sent me… here," I grit through my teeth. I can't let him off the hook so easily.

Sighing, Thelios folds his arms and throws his head back. He looks exhausted; his skin is more pale than usual, and his normally taut frame is thinner than before. If I had to guess, I'd say he hadn't eaten in quite a while. Even worse, he reeks of spirits.

"Syd," he frowns, lifting a thick brow. "I already told you—I sent you here because part of me knew us being kin meant very little to me. I figured if I sent you away, I'd keep my hands off you."

Circling where he stands, I watch the nervous twitch on the side of his mouth as he plucks his fingers at his side—a very normal response when he's trying to avoid his feelings.

"You're only repeating yourself, my lord," I say, giving a hard shove to his shoulder. He turns to see me, but I move with the wind to his opposite side before he can catch me. "I want to know why you sent me *here*!" I counter. "To this place!"

Shaking his head, Thelios swipes a dismissive hand through the air. "I am the Grim lord, Sydney. I send folk into my mirth. That is my lot."

"Into your mirth, yes," I hiss, taking a step closer. "I want to know why you sent me *here!*" I shout, stomping my foot against the floor and summoning my scythe to my hand.

As I do so, the murky chasm around us rolls like the tide until we're standing on black, sandy shores.

Gasping, Thelios' eyes grow wide as he looks around in shock. "But how–how did we get here? What dark magic did you invoke?"

Shrugging my shoulders, I shake my head. "Alas, my lord, I have no dark magic to speak of. We are only here at your will. Only you can answer that question."

Turning about, Thelios seems both surprised and comforted by what he sees. "I sent you to my C.O.R.," he mutters, his eyes now glassy dark pools.

A few tears fall down my face, but I'm thankful my covering conceals me. "Yes, my lord. You sent me to the place you feel most safe. Why, my lord Grim? If you were so disgusted by taking up with me, if the thought of me, a wretch, sickened you so—why would you bring me here?"

"Because I love you!" Thelios shouts back, his eyes flashing black as night before returning to their violent emerald hue.

Exhaling, I grab my waist, finally breathing again. I feel like I've been holding my breath since the moment he arrived.

Snorting, I wipe my face, turning away from him. "Well, you have quite a ridiculous way of showing it, my lord." I head toward the tall stone wall; tracing my fingers along the cool slate, I sigh, thankful the truth is finally out there. "While it doesn't feel like I've been here long, I know I've been here long enough. On occasion, I'd run my hand along the stone, wondering if I'd see my name, but I didn't. I'd see others, but never my own. If the Grim lord sent me into his mirth, surely my name would be here—unless he didn't want to remember me. A vile creature like Purcival could make the cut, but not me!" I chided, laughing and crying all the same.

"Sydney," Thelios begins, hovering behind me. I feel his hands wave over my shoulder, but he backs away, knowing it's too soon to touch me. "I suppose there's a better part of me, a part that knows to protect you, to keep you safe. That's the part that sent you here, the part that would never hurt you."

Turning around to see his crestfallen face and tearful gaze, I shove his chest with my palms. "And what part of you is here now?"

"The better part." Thelios smiles his perfectly crooked calavera grin. It's the same haughty grin that had me leaking from my breasts to my core when I first entered his suite, the same perfectly crooked grin I saw when he stopped Calis from striking me down when I bombarded his courtyard, and it's the same endearing smile warming my heart right now.

I rip my hood off, wanting to see if that same smile remains. I need to know if he's just as sickened as the first time I removed my hood. I always knew taking it off could change things between us if he didn't like what he saw, and now I'll know for sure.

Slowly, Thelios' hands carefully trail up my arms, to my neck, along my jawline. The smooth black tip of his thumb etches the half calavera outline of my mouth before gingerly tracing the darkened circle around my eye.

"Beautiful," he breathes, a sweet smile cresting over his typical smug and sexy grin. "We're the same now," he whispers, his gaze sweeping over me in one fluid stroke, only to settle dead level with my eyes. "But these," Thelios groans in a dark, haunting tone, "these are what I've been waiting to see. I knew they would be beautiful," he adds, drifting his finger along the crevice of my eyes. "One green like mine," he smiles, "and the other—"

"Like lightning–just like my mother, Lorna. She was the Grim," I admit shyly, lowering my head.

Still holding my face, he lifts it back up to meet his eyes. "When did you know?"

Fidgeting with my fingers, I smile. "When I put the ring on, it all became clear. That's why my father kept it for safekeeping, I suppose."

Pulling me into his embrace, Thelios kisses the top of my head. "I'm so sorry, Sydney. I should not have put you through this alone."

I want to hate him. I should, but I cannot. Every fiber of my being is drawn to every toxic fiber of his, and I want to thread myself through his web until we are tethered as one.

Hitting his chest again with my fist, I cry, "Never do that again!"

Laughing darkly, Thelios pulls away from me. "Fucking Fates!" he belts, shaking his head in amusement. "Now it all makes sense."

"What? I ask, curious.

"*Mea Tenebris Eternus Amor*. My dark eternal love. That's who you are, Syd. Who you were always meant to be. My endless, dark, eternal love."

# CHAPTER 50

"Is that who I am?" Sydney huffs, pushing me away, lifting her scythe to my chin.

Wincing as the tip of her blade pierces my flesh, I bite my lip to stay calm. "Yes, Sydney, that is who you are to me," I wholly admit as I feel her dig the blade in deeper.

Sydney's eyes darken to an almost hollow black, resembling my more grimly features, and my chest swells with pride. She is perfect, born of Night and glistening with darkness, and I love her. Her eyes return to a striking heterochromia, revealing her respective green and silver irises. I can tell she's still not sure if she can trust me, and I don't blame her.

My eyes stay trained on Sydney as she holds the scythe at my jugular, wholly entranced by her now more than ever before. For so long, I thought that without a fleshy lump lodged within my chest, I had no heart. Now, I know that a heart is so much more. Sydney alone wields the blade that is my heart—herself. Only she can dig where others dare not tread.

"I should cut your throat for everything you put me through!" she yells, digging a little deeper.

I grunt out my agreement. "Cut deeper, dear. I owe you blood."

"You deserve hell!" she sneers, black tears rolling down her chin.

Sydney's glassy eyes lock with mine as she screams, a high, wailing cry fitting for a Specter. With my eyes open and my feet planted, I hold my ground. If this is to be my end, it'll be to the sound of her voice alone.

Yet, I'm amazed as I'm left standing, unaffected by her hallowing glare. "Being without you is hell enough," I confess.

Dropping her scythe to the ground without warning, Sydney suddenly pulls my face to hers, crashing our mouths together.

I didn't know how much I needed her kiss until now. As her tongue collides with mine, dark electricity rivets through our bodies, connecting us as one. Swirling, twisting, and tasting, Sydney and I kiss as if our worlds collided, and it's everything I need.

"Don't you ever give up on us again," Sydney moans into our kiss, owning this moment as she forces me to the wall.

"Never," I growl back, running my hand through her wavy black hair, and I wince when I feel sharp teeth tear into my wrist. Looking over Sydney's shoulder, I'm surprised to find two small snakes lashing their forked tongues out at me.

"Well hello there," I coo before kissing her mouth and neck so desperately, I feel faint.

"Hold still," she orders, planting a hard kiss on my mouth before backing away.

As she does, she slowly removes her cloak, revealing her perfect naked body beneath. Just as lovely as before, she stands in front of me perfected with tethered serpents delicately laced throughout her skin. I want to ask her if she's named them yet, but the dark look in her eyes tells me to remain quiet.

I want to rush to her, throw her down, and drive my hard length into her sweet, slick center, but when I feel my arms and neck slammed to the wall behind me, I'm shocked to see shadowy hands holding me steady. I narrow my eyes, enchanted by the alluring gaze she's giving me in return.

"Let me introduce you to my shadow." Sydney's haunting tone is melodic, sweeping over me as her shadows gracefully glide over my body. My britches are yanked down causing Sydney's eyes to travel to my waist, clearly pleased to see me hard and ready for her. "Now, let's see if I can charm the most venomous of them all." She smirks as her shadows lift her from the ground, and she wraps her legs around my waist, connecting us as one.

~

"Thelios, are you sure about this?" Sydney winces, her petite palm trembling in mine.

Lifting her chin and turning her to face me, I smile. "You are my endless, dark, eternal love. I couldn't be more sure about anything. Now, just trust me."

Sydney's lips crest into a small smile that reaches her eyes. "I trust you," she breathes back.

I plant a soft kiss on her wrist before removing her grim ring. Placing it in her palm, I give her nod. "Okay, when I give the go ahead, we'll both place our rings in the skull."

"What will happen?" Her eyes stare up at me full of wonder.

Pursing my lips, I shrug. "I'm not sure, but I have a feeling it will all make sense."

Taking a deep breath, Sydney offers another grin, squaring her shoulders some and preparing for what happens next.

Swallowing down whatever remains of my angst, I motion for us to lift our rings toward the skull. Once more, I glance at the inscription: *Mea Tenebris Eternus Amor*. Until now I've never given much thought to what the words inscribed on the grimskull meant. I inherited many artifacts like this one when I took up the mantle as Grim Lord.

One final nod and we insert our rings inside the grimskull.

As we do, black and gray clouds swirl around us as a fiery mist falls upon our skin. Shimmering, flaming embers dance across the sky as shadowy hands pull Sydney and I close. Sydney and I lock our hands together and our serpent familiars coil around our wrists binding us as one.

Our eyes pinned to one another, I now see in Sydney the one thing I never thought I'd find: hope. A spring of hope wells within me as images of the life we're meant to live flash vividly before my eyes.

Sydney isn't just my woman. She is my fate and the only one capable of filling the hollow hole of my heart.

Looking at her, I only hope to see what is revealed before me now.

I see us. Together. Forever. *Always.*

# Epilogue

"Come on already," Thelios sighs. "I've aged a thousand years, woman!"

"Patience, patience!" Pella buzzes, flying past Thelios and Roark. Roark only laughs in return, shaking his head, patting his fellow death dealer's shoulder.

"She's almost ready!" Hala yells back.

Thelios throws up his hands in frustration. "Must it take this long, really?"

Prince Kharon laughs, his shoulders rolling forward in amusement. "Just wait until she's picking out wedding gowns." He throws a nod toward Lady Rae.

Shrieking, Thelios rears his head back in frustration. "Please, sire! One thing at a time!"

"Don't tease him, Khar," Lady Rae calls from the top step of the Soleil.

Grumbling playfully, the prince shrugs his shoulders. "Well, if the Grim lord learned to harness his skill in the Soleil, he could do this himself."

"Yes," Roark agrees. "Now, you're left to Oru and Gao's devices."

"And they just love to put on a big show," Prince Kharon laughs heartily.

A blaze of fire shoots out from the side of the tent before a flash of light. Looking up, his eyes wide with admiration, Thelios drops his jaw at the sight of Lorna Sydney now standing atop the landing.

A mixture of passion and promise hold him captive as he regards her; the newly charged Grim-regent of Purgia. Prince Kharon decreed Lorna-Sydney as Grim-regent just days ago. Knowing he isn't merely relegated to his company of shadows, but he now has Sydney to stand at his side, fills him with hope and joy.

Gracefully sauntering down the platform, one long leg in front of the other, Sydney wears a velvety red cloak with ornate black etching. Adorned in a red and black tunic with a long slit showcasing the serpent familiars along her calf, she is a sight to behold.

Thelios offers his hand as she reaches the landing and she places her hand in his, smiling sweetly as everyone gazes at her in admiration.

"Beautiful," Thelios whispers, planting a small kiss on the calavera side of her face.

"Absolutely stunning!" Lady Rae smiles as she and Pella clap joyfully at the base of the stairs.

Hala and Liv remain at the top of the steps, both girls giggling as they watch.

"Well, Prince Kharon," Roark begins, clearing his throat. "What do you think of these two?"

Lifting his brow, the prince saunters to the middle of the Soleil. Extending his hand toward Lady Rae, he smiles as he slides his gaze over Thelios and Sydney.

"These two?" He laughs a little. "Oh, it's not just these two. It's the whole lot of us. The Ferryman. The Grim. The Reaper. Completed by something none of us sought to find—*love*. Now that we have it, I know one thing: we'll set the world ablaze to keep it."

And the
darkly e

lived

after.

# *First Comes Vengeance...*
## THEN A REVIEW

Thanks for reading Vengeance Born! Now spread the word by leaving a review on my direct site and Goodreads. You can also use this QR code to find my curated playlist on Spotify and find my other books or subscribe to my newsletter.

# More from L.C. Son

Explore the books and short stories of the Beautiful Nightmare Universe:

Books

Beautiful Nightmare (Book One)

Hearts Eclipsed, A Beautiful Nightmare Novella

Awaken: Beautiful Nightmare (Book Two)

Untamed: A Beautiful Nightmare Story

Beta Rising

One Winter's Kiss: A Beautiful Nightmare Story

Fire Kissed & Fire Born Duet (Netherworld Series Debut)

Coming Soon

Vengeance Born: A Grim & Reaper Netherworld Tale

Beautifully Dark Things- Planned 2024

Dawn of Descent: Beautiful Nightmare (Book Three) TBA

Short Stories

I AM NO WITCH: A Beautiful Nightmare Short Story

With Clipped Wings of Butterflies: A Beautiful Nightmare Short Story

With Hearts Like Fire: A Beautiful Nightmare Short Story

For more info on my books, visit:

My Books & Short Stories - L. C. Son Books (lcsonbooks.com)

Remember leaving reviews makes you an MVP!!

Thank you!

# About L.C. Son

Known for her Amazon Best Seller *One Winter's Kiss*, and the series starter, and epic fantasy novel, *Beautiful Nightmare (Book One)*, L.C. Son is the happy wife of more than twenty years to her high school sweetheart and a loving mom of three.

Growing up, she spent hours reading comic books she "borrowed" from her older brother, which inspired her love of heroes and all things fantasy and paranormal. Much like the characters she adored, she lives a duplicitous life. By day, she works tirelessly to champion the employment of persons with severe disabilities. By night, she puts on her wife-mom cape, sharing with her husband at their church and juggling their kids' highly active schedules.

Presently, she's working on the next installment of monsters, myths, and misfits.

For the latest info and to join the member-only newsletter, visit: www.lcsonbooks.com.

www.ingramcontent.com/pod-product-compliance
Lightning Source LLC
Chambersburg PA
CBHW061242310726
48971CB00007B/2177